APESHIT

Also by Carlton Mellick III

Satan Burger
Electric Jesus Corpse
Sunset With a Beard   (stories)
Razor Wire Pubic Hair
Teeth and Tongue Landscape
The Steel Breakfast Era
The Baby Jesus Butt Plug
Fishy-fleshed
The Menstruating Mall
Ocean of Lard   (with Kevin L. Donihe)
Punk Land
Sex and Death in Television Town
Sea of the Patchwork Cats
The Haunted Vagina
Cancer-cute   (Avant Punk Army Exclusive)
War Slut
Sausagey Santa
Ugly Heaven, Beautiful Hell   (with Jeffrey Thomas)
Adolf in Wonderland
Ultra Fuckers
Cybernetrix
The Egg Man

APESHIT

CARLTON MELLICK III

AVANT PUNK

AVANT PUNK

AN IMPRINT OF ERASERHEAD PRESS

ERASERHEAD PRESS
205 NE BRYANT
PORTLAND, OR 97211

WWW.ERASERHEADPRESS.COM

ISBN: 1-933929-76-6

Printed in the USA.

Author's Note

I was always into low budget horror movies. The crappier they are the better. After I played an insane priest in the low budget horror movie *The Ancient*, I really wanted to write a screenplay for my own crappy low budget horror movie. Why the hell not? The typical cliché involving a group of teenagers in the woods getting killed off one at a time for some reason or another is my personal favorite. I wanted to do something like that, yet give it a little twist. You know, like where it turns out that the crazy supernatural killer in the forest won't die because instead of internal organs he's filled with a bunch of corndogs, and the only way to kill him for good is to eat all the corndogs out of him, but none of the characters are all that hungry because they just ate some sandwiches so they've got to get to town and find some fat guy who would be able to eat all the corndogs for them. Of course, that wouldn't be as easy as it sounds because the killer would have this crazy hairdo that is like a mullet but it's also a chainsaw. You know, a Chainsaw Mullet, which is what the movie would be called, and what all the characters would get killed with in horrible yet interesting ways. Now that I think about it, that sounds like a pretty awesome movie. I should have written that one instead.

The movie I planned to do was called *Apeshit*. Although I never got around to writing the screenplay, I did turn the idea into this book. I figured if any director likes this book then I'll just write the screenplay for them later.

Writing this book was a guilty pleasure, like Cybernetrix or The Haunted Vagina. It's not "serious" literature, but I approached a goofy idea as seriously as I could. Somebody once told me that the goofiest ideas often make the best stories. I'm not sure if I agree with that, but I sure like writing goofy stories like The Faggiest Vampire, Sausagey Santa, and The Morbidly Obese Ninja (forthcoming).

The problem with starting a book with a goofy idea is that they rarely end up as comedies. Apeshit isn't as goofy as I wanted it to be. In fact, it's pretty fucked up. I didn't want to write something so fucked up, but I guess I really couldn't control the story. It wanted to go in its own direction. Harlan Ellison claims that his characters will often take on lives of their own. He wants them to go one way, but they want to go another. They take over his stories and write themselves whether he likes it or not. That's kind of what happened to me while writing Apeshit. The story went in directions I didn't want it to go and I couldn't do anything to stop it. I asked this story, "What the fuck is wrong with you?" and it just flipped me off and went on with its business. This book surely is not the most fucked up book ever written, it wasn't supposed to be, but it's fucked up enough. Part of me doesn't actually want anybody to read it.

I'm guessing people are going to accuse me of trying to be "shocking for the sake of being shocking" with this book. More so than any of my previous books. But this couldn't be farther from the truth. A few weeks ago, I was talking to Chuck Palahniuk about the whole "shocking for the sake of being shocking" thing, because both of us are regularly accused of doing this. I told him that I'm just trying to be interesting for the sake of being interesting. Whether I succeed or fail at being interesting, that's up to the reader to decide, but I've never tried to shock anyone with my work. I didn't think anyone was actually shocked by anything anymore. Chuck said that what some people view as interesting other people view as shocking. But shock fades with time. Eventually, people will see what is interesting about things that used to be shocking.

It really doesn't matter, though. It's best to just write for yourself and not worry too much about what other people think. Everybody is going to think you're just full of shit anyway. All writers are full of shit. I wish we were full of corndogs instead, but we're just not.

- Carlton Mellick III, 08/23/08 1:56 pm

CHAPTER ONE
DESDEMONA

Desdemona is the only girl on the cheerleading squad with a mohawk. It is normally colored white with red tips—because red and white are the school colors—but she wants to try a new color for their weekend in the mountains.

"What do you think: green, blue, or purple?" Desdemona asks Crystal, holding up three cans of hair dye with her colorfully tattooed fingers. She is also the only girl on the cheerleading squad with a full body suit of tattoos.

Crystal sighs at the cans of hair dye. It has been over five weeks, but she still hasn't accepted her best friend's latest choice of hairstyle.

"Green, I guess," Crystal says. She drops her eyes to an abortion information website on her laptop. "At least it will match your eyes."

"You're right!" Desdemona says. "This is going to be sooo cute!"

She smiles wide as she finishes shaving the sides of her head with her dad's mustache clippers. Then she reads the instructions on the back of the hair dye bottle, blinking her long black eyelashes rapidly.

"Punk isn't a cute style," Crystal says.

"Stop calling my style punk! It doesn't mean I'm punk just because I've got a mohawk."

"Nobody has mohawks except for the punks," Crystal says, cleaning her laptop keys with a Handi Wipe. "People are starting to think you're one of them."

"But look at my clothes. I would never wear punk clothes."

Crystal shakes her head. "You think that matters to them?"

"I think mohawks are pretty," Desdemona says. She looks at herself in her vanity mirror, caressing the smooth bald sides of her head. "And feminine."

"You're crazy," Crystal says.

"Not as crazy as you," Desdemona says.

Crystal and Desdemona are the richest, prettiest, snobbiest, most popular girls in school. They are captain and co-captain of the cheerleading squad. They only date the richest, cutest, toughest, most popular boys on the football team. They are the queens of the school. They are the preppiest of the preppies. That's why everyone thought it was so odd when Desdemona wanted to get so many tattoos and a mohawk.

The tattoos happened quickly. At first, she only wanted a blue butterfly tattoo on her left hip. Everyone thought it was hot. Then she wanted a red butterfly on her right hip. Everyone thought it was kind of cool how they matched. Then she tattooed large butterfly wings across the majority of her back. Everyone thought it was big. Then she was addicted. She got a new butterfly tattoo every few days, a variety of different sizes, shapes, and colors. She stopped paying attention to what everyone thought about them. Before anyone knew what was going on, Desdemona had covered every inch of her skin with butterflies. Even her hands, feet, neck, and private areas.

She thought they were pretty. Everyone else thought they were weird.

She charged them all to her daddy's credit card, but he hasn't noticed the charges nor the tattoos yet. He has asked her why she's always wearing gloves and turtleneck sweaters indoors in the middle of spring, but he hasn't pushed the issue. He doesn't even pay attention to all of the lame excuses she makes up.

Crystal tried to stop her from tattooing too much, but couldn't get through to her. It's not easy to stop an addict. Now that Desdemona has the mohawk, Crystal is worried that it is ruining her friend's popularity. She is worried that her own popularity might be in jeopardy for associating with a punk rocker. Crystal is seriously considering breaking off their friendship. She plans to make a decision on this matter after they get back from the cabin.

Once Desdemona finishes her mohawk, gets dressed, does her nails, packs her bags, perfects her makeup, and smokes a couple of mint cigarettes, they take

Crystal's car over to Jason's house.

On the way, they pick up a drive-thru milkshake at the local Steak 'n Shake. They get vanilla. Crystal only likes vanilla. After they each take a few sips, they toss the leftovers at a couple of emo girls walking down the sidewalk in Jason's neighborhood. The emo girls flip them off, their black dresses coated in white goo like a giant bird had pooped on them. Des and Crystal laugh at them and wave goodbye. They love pissing off the goths and the emos.

They arrive at the biggest house in the neighborhood: Jason's house. Everyone else is already there, loading up the van. Des and Crystal check each other's makeup as they enter the driveway. They are made up exactly the same. Their clothes and jewelry are exactly the same. If it wasn't for Des's green mohawk and tattoos, they would be identical.

Just last year, everyone used to think they were twins. They both had platinum blond hair of equal length. They always wore the same clothes and same makeup style. The only way people could tell them apart was that Crystal had blue eyes and wider breasts, and Des had green eyes and pointier breasts. It's extremely easy to tell them apart now.

"You're late," Jason howls at them as they get out of the car.

"Des took forever," Crystal says.

Crystal kisses the air next to Jason's cheek. Desdemona kisses Kevin and Rick. Everyone notices Des's mohawk has been dyed green but none of them comment on it. They pretend that it doesn't exist, just as they always pretend her tattoos don't exist.

"Ready for a weekend of sex, drugs, and alcohol?" Jason says, holding a pony keg of beer over his freckled shoulder and trying to pretend that it's no big deal.

"Hell yeah!" his buddies shout back while shooting hoops.

Desdemona unloads her bags from Crystal's car and tosses them at Kevin and Rick so they can pack them into the van. Kevin and Rick ignore her. They are getting serious over their game of one-on-one. Kevin slams the ball into the basket and yells, "Booyah!" She is pissed they aren't offering to help; she's even more pissed that they haven't complimented her on her new green mohawk.

"Where's Stephanie?" Crystal asks.

"In the bathroom," Jason says. "She's been in there since she got here."

"What's she doing in there?" Crystal asks.

"I think she's sick," he says.

"Great," Crystal says. "Is she going to crap out on us again?"

"I hope so," Jason says. "It would be a lot more fun without her."

Stephanie is in the bathroom, crying. She has been crying all day. She really doesn't want to go on the trip, but she's thankful she'll be able to get away from home for a while. She's not allowed to cry at home.

Crystal knocks on the door.

Stephanie sucks in her breath and holds it, trying to stop herself from crying. She doesn't want Crystal to know she's having problems. She doesn't want to have to explain herself.

"Hey, Steph," Crystal says. "Are you okay in there?"

Stephanie takes a couple deep breaths. Crystal can hear her breathing.

"I'll be fine," Stephanie says, blowing her nose.

"You don't have the flu or anything, do you?"

"No," Stephanie says, fixing her black curly hair in the mirror. "I'm just . . . hungover."

"Was there a party last night? Why didn't you invite me?"

"I was just drinking with Dan." Her voice cracks a little when she says *Dan*.

Crystal realizes that something else is going on. Stephanie never hangs out with her older brother anymore, especially when he's drinking. Dan gets way too violent and crazy when he drinks. After that time he tried to hit her with his car, Stephanie vowed never to drink with him again.

Dan used to be a part of their group of friends. He used to be the one who bought them beer. But nobody likes Dan anymore. He's a pathetic asshole. The more his life sucks, the bigger the asshole he becomes. And his life is 360 degrees of suck. He works a shitty job, he drives a shitty car, he still lives with his parents, he can't get a girlfriend to save his life, all of his friends moved away after high school, he doesn't have any hobbies or goals, he's addicted to meth, and he knows he's just a big waste of space. Stephanie can't handle being around him. She wishes that he'd go back to jail.

Crystal doesn't push the issue. She knows Stephanie has major emotional issues and that she doesn't like to talk about them. She knows that Steph prefers to keep that kind of stuff hidden deep inside of her so that she can pretend it doesn't exist. Stephanie's good at hiding things. You wouldn't realize she had such painful emotional problems if you ever saw her cheer. She is the happiest, most excited, energetic cheerleader on the squad. She's a really good actress.

When Stephanie opens the door, Crystal says, "Let's go have a fun weekend."

Stephanie smiles wide and says, "I can't wait!"

After the van is packed, they all cram themselves inside and head for the interstate.

The guys are already drinking. They started the party early. Jason drinks the fastest, even though he's driving. He is already on his fifth Coors.

He says, "Who cares if we crash, it's only a rental."

Crystal has a beer but she is just barely sipping it. She is acting as navigator and more importantly, music controller. Unfortunately, Crystal has the worst taste in music. She always pretends that she listens to whatever is popular at the time, but if you let her plug her ipod into your car stereo she is going to be playing only one kind of music: Korean rap.

"Jesus Christ," Jason says as his girlfriend blasts a goofy song called *Ice-cream* by a goofy Korean rapper named MC Mong. He hates her taste in music.

Lucky for Crystal, Des and her boyfriends find K-rap completely hilarious, especially the group M.H. IS who try really hard to come off as tough ghetto thugs. They dance together in the backseat, bumping their hips together with the music.

Jason doesn't find it funny. He would rather listen to something serious. He likes things that are serious. He asks everyone if they want to listen to something different, but Crystal and the dance party in the back seat are having too much fun. Stephanie is the only one who doesn't care either way.

The hopping and dancing in the backseat causes the van to shake and sway as they get on the interstate. As he dances, Kevin accidentally spills his beer on Desdemona's bare shoulder and then licks it off of her butterfly tattoos before she can get mad at him. Rick accidentally elbows Des in the breast, so she elbows him in the stomach.

After an hour on the road, Des falls asleep on Rick's shoulder and Kevin falls asleep on her shoulder. Rick doesn't sleep, though. He hardly ever sleeps. He stares out of the car window, drinking a beer, caressing his smooth-shaven face.

Rick, Kevin, and Desdemona are in a threesome relationship. Aside from Crystal, nobody knows that Rick and Kevin are bisexual. Jason, Stephanie, and everyone at school thinks Des just has two boyfriends, that they are sharing her, that they take turns being with her. Nobody knows that Rick and Kevin are also romantically involved with each other. Nobody knows that all three of them want to marry each other after high school and start a family together.

The relationship started with Rick and Des. They had been a couple since they were freshmen. Kevin was Rick's best friend. He didn't have a girlfriend. For most of high school, the three of them would hang out. They went to movies together. They went to basketball games together. They went to restaurants together. Kevin thought he was being a third wheel, but Des and Rick assured him that they liked having him around. It wasn't until later that he discovered they wanted him around because they were both attracted to him.

Senior year, Des really wanted to dump Rick for Kevin. She thought Kevin was more interesting and confident than Rick. Even though Rick had a tough guy personality around his friends, Des thought he was too sensitive and needy in private. She thought he was more attractive than Kevin, but Kevin had the better personality.

During a homecoming party, Kevin was drunk and flirted heavily with Desdemona. They ended up sleeping together while Rick was passed out in his car. The next day, Kevin told Rick everything. He said he was drunk and would never try to steal Desdemona away from him. Des apologized as well. Rick forgave Kevin right away, because Kevin meant a lot to him, but he told Des that he wouldn't forgive her unless she let him sleep with another woman. Desdemona refused. Rick said that it was only fair and that she was being a bitch. She said it would only be fair if he slept with Kevin. This created an awkward silence.

Desdemona knew Rick was bisexual. He never told her, but she had been with him long enough to notice when he was checking out guys. Kevin was not bisexual at the time, but he also wasn't straight, nor was he gay. Kevin was more asexual back then. He wasn't really attracted to anyone. He didn't date. He didn't chase women. The only reason he flirted with Desdemona was because he was drunk and really horny. He lost his virginity to Des that night in the bathroom at the homecoming party. After they had sex, Kevin realized he liked women.

When Desdemona suggested Rick sleep with Kevin, all three of them could tell that Rick liked the idea. He started to blush and diverted his eyes.

Kevin did not like the idea. He knew Des was only joking, but he didn't think it was a very funny joke. Kevin was best friends with Rick. They had been friends since they were kids. During that awkward silence, Kevin knew that his friendship with Rick would never be the same.

Kevin was the one to break the silence.

He said, "I think it's a good idea."

Rick said, "Really?"

Kevin didn't want to have sex with his best friend. He was not attracted to men, but he wasn't really disgusted by them either. The reason he agreed to do it was because he was worried about losing his friend. He didn't want to hurt Rick's feelings by refusing him. After they had sex, Kevin realized he liked men as well.

That's when the three of them started sleeping together. At first, Kevin was more like a fuck buddy for them. He was something that improved their sex life, but he wasn't romantically involved with them. After they had sex, Kevin would go home and wouldn't take part in the after-sex snuggles. But Des and Rick soon fell in love with Kevin, and then Kevin fell in love with Des and Rick. It wasn't long before they were all committed to each other.

18

They take an exit off of the interstate onto a small country highway. They stop at a rundown, dumpster-smelling, faded yellow country store to get some gas, eat some candy bars, and use the bathrooms.

"There's nothing else until we get there," Jason says, eating a spicy pickle as he pumps the gas. "We're still about an hour away."

Kevin smokes a cigarette in response, rubbing his shaved head. He kicks the window of the van to wake up Rick in the backseat, to no avail. Rick is dead asleep with his hand down his pants, fingering his crotch with wet fingers, having nice dreams.

Desdemona is leaning against the van, flipping off some local redneck at the next pump. The local is an older man with a titanic beer gut and a crooked chin, whose face is permanently stuck in a frowning expression. Des doesn't like him staring at her with his creepy look. She thinks he is ogling her ass and checking out the tattooed cleavage hanging out of her tank top, but he's really giving her a dirty look because he doesn't approve of her mohawk.

"What in the hell happened to your head?" says the redneck.

The mohawked girl doesn't understand what he means. She says, "Go fuck yourself."

The redneck gets into his truck. As he drives away, he says, "If you were my daughter I'd beat the devil out of you."

Kevin charges the truck and throws his cigarette at the driver's side door. Then he raises his middle finger as high as he can. The redneck doesn't even notice he's there, but Des appreciates the gesture. She wraps her arm around his waist and kisses him on the side of his shaved head.

"Better watch out," Jason tells them. "Piss off the wrong rednecks and they might go Deliverance on your ass."

"I'll go Deliverance on *their* asses!" Desdemona says.

Kevin laughs. "I'm sure you would."

"I'm actually serious," Jason says. "There's supposed to be some weird little town up here somewhere that's filled with a bunch of scary ass rednecks. My dad and my uncle came out here once on a fishing trip, a long time ago, probably before I was born. My dad said they came across this freaky derelict town in the middle of nowhere, filled with nothing but dirty inbred retards."

Desdemona recoils at the word *retard*. She's sensitive to the word because she used to babysit a man with Down syndrome. She's not offended by the term, but whenever she hears it she remembers that man and how sad his life was. He was trapped in a child's mind, watching cartoons and playing with stuffed animals all day. His parents were practically too old to take care of him. It was the most depressing household she had ever seen.

"We totally have to go there," Kevin says.

"Fuck no," Jason says. "My dad said they're so inbred that they've got giant lumpy faces and teeth growing out of their noses."

"In that case, we're *definitely* going," Kevin says.

"I'm telling you," Jason says. "You don't fuck around with those kinds of rednecks."

Kevin laughs. "What are you talking about? Inbred mutant hillbillies know how to party!"

Jason laughs, but Desdemona doesn't think it's funny. She gets serious about the issue.

"There's no inbred mutants," Desdemona says.

"Yes, there is," Jason says. "My dad's told the story a hundred times."

"I'm sure he was just exaggerating," Desdemona says. "Even if they were really inbred, it doesn't mean they were all deformed mutants."

"But they were!"

"Your dad's just putting you on. Inbreeding causes a lot of problems, but I doubt it creates sideshow freaks."

"Of course it does!" Jason says.

Desdemona takes a beer from the backseat and drinks it while shaking her head. Jason opens his mouth to argue further but is interrupted by the gas station door swinging open. Crystal and Stephanie step out, carrying taffy, zingers, and a big bag of pork rinds.

"Let's get out of here," Crystal says. "This place smells like ass."

The small country highway is about as empty as highways come. There doesn't seem to be anything or anyone out here. They see old trucks passing them every once in awhile, but they have no idea where they are coming from.

"I fucking hate rednecks," Desdemona says.

Kevin rubs her shoulder. "Don't worry, Rick will protect you from the rednecks."

Desdemona looks down at Rick. His mouth is wide open against the side of the van and drool is leaking down the window. Even the blasting of Korean Rap music won't wake him up.

"What about you?" she asks Kevin. "Won't you protect me?"

"Are you kidding?" he says. "First sign of a crazy mutant redneck and I'm fucking out of there."

"What!" she shoves him with her bare feet.

"You're on your own!"

Desdemona shakes her head at him and laughs.

The farther up the mountain they go, the more roadkill they pass. At first, the roadkill is only small birds and squirrels. Down a ways, they find dead rabbits, dead snakes, dead skunks, and dead possum. Stephanie counts the dead animals they pass. She wonders why so many of them have been run over on such a sparsely driven highway.

The road becomes bumpy. It has fallen into disrepair here, crumbled, cracked. The forest is trying to take back the highway. There is even more roadkill here, and Stephanie is surprised at the various species of dead animals that they pass. They are not your typical roadkill. They pass a dead porcupine, a dead weasel, dead goats, dead bats, dead pigs, a dead turkey, a dead beaver, a dead hawk, a dead peacock. Stephanie didn't even know that all of these types of animals lived in this part of the country.

"Oh, my god," Stephanie says, as she sees something up ahead.

The others see it, too.

The highway up ahead is so dense with roadkill that the dead bodies are in piles covering the road. There are dozens of animal corpses here, most of them too mutilated to recognize.

"What the fuck?" Jason says.

"Holy shit." Crystal nearly knocks the beer out of Jason's hand as she points at the biggest pile of bodies. It is nearly five feet high.

Desdemona wakes up Rick so that he can check this out.

"This isn't roadkill," Stephanie says. "Something else is going on."

"It's like something else killed them," Crystal says. "Like pollution or radiation."

"Or some crazy redneck with an automatic rifle," Jason says.

They drive slowly through the bodies. Whenever they roll over an animal corpse and they feel the side of the van raise, Crystal and Desdemona cringe.

"It's like the fucking apocalypse," Kevin says.

As the smell hits them, they all cover their noses with their shirts and roll up the windows.

"There's probably some reasonable explanation for it," Desdemona says.

"Like what?" Jason says.

"Because of the variety of animals, I bet it has to do with taxidermy," Des replies. "Probably some taxidermist that lives up here drove down this bumpy road with his pickup truck filled with dead animals he planned to stuff. He probably didn't secure them properly and they spilled out of the back of his truck."

"Bullshit," Jason says.

"It sounds reasonable to me," Crystal says.

But the farther up they drive, the less they believe Desdemona's explanation. Because up ahead, the animals are bigger. They pass a few dead deer, a dead cow, and a dead black bear.

"He could have had a big truck . . ." Desdemona says.

"No way," Jason says. "This is something far more fucked up."

Desdemona says, "Well, it's obvious that these things didn't all die here. Somebody either put them here on purpose or dropped them here by accident. Perhaps some hunter without a permit dumped them here and—"

Des stops talking when she sees the hunter. There is a man with a rifle in a hunting outfit, lying twisted in the dirt on the side of the road. He is not moving and is covered in blood.

They keep their shirts over their noses as they step out of the van and approach the body. Stephanie and Rick stay in their seats. Rick is too nervous and Stephanie is too sick. Steph is extremely sensitive to smells and is already on the verge of throwing up. Her face is in her lap as she focuses on holding back the vomit, gagging and drooling a little. The others can't stop themselves from checking it out.

The dead man's face is busted open. His nose is a scabby pulp. His limbs are curled backwards. Chunks of meat are threaded into his bushy black beard. It looks like he was hit by a truck or beaten to death by a dozen baseball bats. There are flies crawling across his face and something squirming beneath his skin. It looks like he has been dead for days.

"Jesus Christ," Desdemona says.

"He's fucked up," Jason says.

"You think?" Desdemona says.

"What's moving under his skin?" Kevin says from behind them, casually drinking a beer and eating a pork rind. "Are those maggots?"

When Stephanie hears the word maggots she opens the door and pukes on the road. Kevin laughs at her, but nobody else thinks it's funny. They are all on the verge of puking themselves.

"I'm going to call the cops," Crystal says, pulling out her cell phone and walking around to the other side of the van.

"What do you think happened to him?" Jason asks.

"Same thing as these animals, I guess," Desdemona says.

Desdemona leans in for a closer look at his wounds. She covers her nose as tightly as she can. Then she puts her tennis shoe against the corpse and tries to flip him over onto his back.

"What the hell are you doing?" Jason cries. "This is a fucking crime scene. Don't move the body."

She ignores Jason and continues to push on the body until it flips over. Once it falls on its back, the smell in the air becomes twice as pungent and the flies leap into a buzzing whirlwind. There were more flies on him than they realized. Jason backs away. He doesn't want to be touched by any of the flies that had been on the dead body.

There are two holes in the dead man's torso.

"Are those bullet holes?" Kevin says.

"I told you," Jason says. "There's fucking crazy red-necks out here. They probably shot him."

Desdemona kneels down next to the body. "They're too wide and shallow to be bullet holes. They are also too symmetrical."

"What do you think happened?" Kevin asks. He chugs the rest of his beer and then tosses the can at the dead bear.

"I think he was just hit by a truck," Desdemona says.

"And those holes in his chest?" Jason asks.

"Probably from some kind of hood ornament," she replies. "Like bull horns."

"What are you, an expert in forensics or something?" Jason asks.

"She just thinks she is," Kevin says. "She watches a lot of cop shows."

Desdemona turns and looks up at them. "I think I'd be good in forensics. I totally want to do this kind of stuff professionally."

"You?" Jason says. "Professionals don't kick the bodies over."

Kevin laughs.

Desdemona makes a pissy face at them and then turns back to the corpse to examine it further. When she looks down, she realizes that the corpse is no longer on its back. It has propped itself up and is looking at Desdemona with its smashed-in face. The dead man is still alive.

He moans at Desdemona and grabs her by the ankle, squeezing as tight as he can with blood-crusted fingers. Des-demona screams. She falls to the ground and crawls back-wards, but the man won't let go of her ankle.

"He's still alive!" Desdemona cries. "He's still fucking alive!"

"Holy fuck!" Jason says, stepping away from them.

Kevin lunges at the half-dead hunter. He tries to separate the man's fingers from Des's ankle but the grip is too tight. Flakes of skin come off in Kevin's hand.

"Get off this land," the hunter says with a dry, croaking voice. "You don't belong here."

Maggots crawl on his tongue as he speaks. The smell coming out of his mouth is so rancid that both Kevin and Des have to turn away. The man crawls through the dirt, trying to get closer.

Rick jumps out of the van. He doesn't realize the man assaulting Des is the same man who was lying there dead earlier. He thinks some crazy person has come out of the woods and attacked her. While running at the man, instinct takes over in Rick. He is the star kicker on the football team and envisions the crazy hunter's head as a football.

The kick connects with such force that it knocks him backwards, breaking his grasp on Des's ankle. Dried blood explodes from the man's head on impact, showering Kevin's shaved head and Desdemona's bare legs with scab dust.

The hunter lands in the dirt and lies there. For a minute, they think that Rick has just killed the man, for real this time. But the hunter gets back up. He pulls himself to his feet.

"I'm warning you," says the hunter with blackened lips. "Get the hell out of here. Just go."

Then he runs off into the woods.

CHAPTER TWO
STEPHANIE

Stephanie is in the van brushing her teeth. She always brushes her teeth whenever she's nervous. She has brushed her teeth five times today already. White foam is drooling out of her mouth onto her knees. Her mind is in another place.

There is a knock at the window. Stephanie snaps out of it. She sees Crystal looking in at her, tapping on the window with her cell phone while she's on hold with the cops. Crystal says *are you okay?* with her eyebrows. Stephanie nods her head and then spits toothpaste out into an empty beer can. She looks out the other window to see if the others are okay. Kevin and Rick are comforting Desdemona. Stephanie can't tell if Des is laughing or crying.

Jason comes around the side of the van just as Crystal gets off the phone.

"Are they coming?" he asks.

"Not for awhile," Crystal says. "They said we don't have to wait around and can keep going if we want. They said they'd call my cell if they needed any extra information."

"That's kind of weird," Jason says.

"The weird part is that the old woman on the phone

31

acted as if she knew all about the dead animals," Crystal says. "As if it happens all the time."

"What about the dead guy?"

"That's even weirder. When I told her there was a dead guy on the side of the road, she didn't seem to really care that much. Once it turned out that the guy wasn't dead, the woman said *oh, that's probably just Alan. He does that all the time.*"

"What the fuck?" Jason says. "What does he do all the time? Get hit by a truck and then lay on the side of the road for hours?"

"I don't know," Crystal says. "She acted like it was no big deal. I even described how messed up he was and she just said, *yeah, he's been needing to go to the hospital for a long time now. I'll send Roy out to pick him up later.*"

"Fucking *weird* rednecks," Jason says.

"Tell me about it," Crystal says.

"So are we going to have to go back home now?" Jason asks Kevin as he approaches.

"Well, *yeah*," Crystal says.

Kevin shrugs. "I don't think so. Why?"

"Nobody's going to want to go to the cabin after that," Crystal says. "Especially Des."

"Des still wants to go," Kevin says.

"Then we should still go," Jason says.

"Fuck no," Crystal says. "It's not safe out here."

"We're still miles away from the cabin," Jason says. "That Alan guy ran in the opposite direction. Plus he's half-dead and I think his eyes were missing. We'll be fine."

"Are you sure?" Crystal asks.

"There's a ton of guns at the cabin," Jason says. "Nobody's going to fuck with us."

Stephanie brushes her teeth again as they drive down the road. She is more shaken up from the incident than any of them, even though she was the only one who stayed in the van the whole time. Everyone else is laughing and joking about it. They all agree, now that it's over, that it was more exciting than scary.

"At first, I thought he was a zombie!" Kevin says.

"Me too!" Desdemona says.

"I thought all the other dead animals were going to get up and attack us, too," Kevin says.

"What do you think's going to happen to him?" Rick says.

"He's dead, for sure," Jason says. "Did you see those wounds? I don't think the poor bastard is going to survive the night."

"It's pretty sad," Desdemona says. "He's sick in the head. He probably doesn't realize that he's so messed up. The cops really should get him help."

"Yeah, but the cops don't give a fuck," Crystal says. "They're probably going to just let him die out there."

"Fucking assholes," Desdemona says.

"Who cares?" Jason says, cracking another beer. "The guy *needs* to die. He needs to be put out of his misery."

"Don't be such a dick," Crystal says. "What if that was your dad out there? Or you out there?"

"I'll never end up like that guy," Jason says.

"You never know," Crystal says.

They turn off the country road onto a dirt path. The terrain is rugged and overgrown with large roots and bushes.

"It's still another five miles," Jason says. "This dirt road winds up the mountain."

"You sure this is a road?" Kevin says. "It doesn't look like it was designed to be driven on."

"This road probably hasn't been driven on for years," Jason says. "The only thing up this way is grampy's cabin and nobody in my family's been up here for a long time. I'm surprised this road is still here at all."

"Is this place some kind of craphole?" Desdemona says. "I'm not going to have to use an outhouse or anything, am I?"

"My grandpa was a rich bastard," Jason says. "The place is pretty sweet. There's a generator, plumbing, heating, he's probably even installed a jacuzzi since the last time I was here."

"When was the last time you came here?" Rick asks.

"Not since I was a kid," Jason says. "My grandpa and my dad stopped speaking to each other years ago. My grandpa was kind of a drunk and said something to my mom that pissed her off. They got into an argument and my dad threw him out on his ass. That was the last time any of us saw him. He died last year and I inherited the cabin. I inherited all of his cool shit. This is the first time anyone's been up here in God knows how long. My dad hasn't seen the place in forever. He refuses to come out here for some reason. I guess he doesn't want to see anything that reminds him of grandpa."

"So you own this place?" Kevin asks.

"Yep," Jason says. "It's all mine."

"*Sweet*," Kevin says.

"Maybe I'll move up here after graduation," Jason says. He looks at Crystal. "What do you think? Want to move out here and be a mountain man with me?"

"Uh, *no*," Crystal says. "I don't *think* so. You can live out here by yourself."

"Come on, it'll be fun," Jason says.

She shakes her head. Jason pinches her thigh.

"Quit it!" she shrieks, as if his pinches were razor-edged.

He pinches her again and smiles.

After a mile, the dirt road gets really rough and steep as it winds up the mountain. They slow down to about five miles per hour. On the left side of the trail, there is a drop-off. It starts off as only about ten feet, but as the road ascends the drop-off becomes twenty, then thirty feet high.

"This looks kind of dangerous," Crystal says, as they ascend another twenty feet.

"Yeah, I was always scared of this part when I was a kid," Jason says. "But I don't remember the road being this thin."

Rick sticks his head out of the window. The left side of the car is so close to the edge of the cliff that he can't see the ground anymore. He looks down. The drop is nearly sixty feet into an ocean of pine trees. There is a loud scraping noise that makes Rick jump and hit the back of his head against the window frame. He looks out of the right window and notices that the other side of the van is only inches away from a rock face. Branches from trees growing out of the earth are scratching across the doors.

"Be careful, Jason," Rick yells over the scraping noise. "We fall off this and we're dead."

"Yeah," Kevin says. "Even if we survive the fall, we'd never be able to get help from way out here."

The scraping is interrupted by a loud *clunk* as a rock jutting out of the ground hits the bottom of the van, bouncing them up and down.

"I've got my cell phone," Crystal says, holding up her phone. "We could just call for a rescue helicopter or something."

She looks at her phone.

"Damn," she says. "There aren't any bars."

"There wouldn't be any bars way out here," Kevin says.

The road gets even thinner. The ground gets rockier and bounces them higher.

"Can you guys shut up," Jason says. "I'm trying to concentrate here."

"You mean we're completely cut off?" Crystal asks.

"Completely," Kevin says, smiling.

At the top of the slope, the path turns right. It heads uphill, away from the cliff. The scraping stops and the road becomes less bumpy.

"We made it!" Kevin says. "Booyah!"

"The way back is the dangerous part," Jason says. "You have to turn at just the right angle or you'll go straight off the cliff. I'll probably need you guys to get out of the van and navigate me."

"Shouldn't you have rented something with four-wheel-drive?" Desdemona asks.

"Nah," Jason says. "My family used to come up here all the time and we never had four-wheel-drive."

"Well, it wouldn't have hurt would it?" Desdemona says.

"I guess it wouldn't have."

After another mile of slow driving through thick

woods, they come to a dead end.

"Here we are," Jason says.

The others look around. They are surrounded by nothing but trees.

"There's nothing here," Crystal says.

"Follow me," Jason says.

They get out of the van and follow Jason through the trees. Kevin stays behind to check out the side of the van and laughs at the large sections of paint that have been stripped away by the trees.

"Ah, *dude*!" Kevin calls, chuckling. "You fucked it up!"

But Jason doesn't care. He just says, "Fuck it."

They take a stone path through the overgrown pine trees until they come to a small clearing. On the other side of the clearing, hidden away from the rest of the world, is the cabin.

It is a lofty three-story wooden structure that looks like it had been designed by Dr. Suess. Its frame is distorted and curved like melted plastic, at least a third of the building is dangling off of a cliff. The wood of the building is weathered and splintered. The windows are caked in mud. Several shingles are missing from the roof. It is dead quiet.

"This place is a dump," Crystal says.

"Yeah," says Desdemona. "I thought this was going to be cool."

"It is cool," Jason says.

"It looks like the cabin from *Evil Dead*," Kevin says. "Only twice as big and twice as freaky."

"It's cool, trust me," Jason says, as he steps onto the porch and puts his key in the door.

The first thing they see when they enter the cabin is hands.

There are dozens of bronzed ornamental hands hanging from the walls of the entry room. They are attached to the walls by the insides of their wrists, appearing as if the hands are reaching out of the wallpaper to grab them.

"What the fuck?" Desdemona says.

"Your grandpa was *weird*," Crystal says.

Jason examines the hands.

"I've never seen these before," he says.

"They're creepy," Desdemona says.

They go into the living room. The walls in here are also covered in hands.

"There used to be deer heads and fish trophies all over these walls," Jason says. "Grampy must have gotten eccentric in his old age."

The house is filled with orange-ish brown and mustard yellow furniture. The wall paper is a shiny copper color. It all looks like it came out of the Seventies. All of the bedrooms are empty except for the master bedroom, which has a queen bed, a nightstand, and a lamp.

"It's changed a lot since I was a kid," Jason says. "I wonder if he redecorated it so that he could rent it out or something."

Jason takes them out on the second floor balcony.

"This is the coolest part," Jason says.

The balcony is huge. Bigger than the living room. It is hanging off of the cliff. It overlooks miles of forest. Not a speck of civilization can be seen.

"The view is amazing," Crystal says. "It's like one of those scenic viewpoints on the highway, but its all our own."

All six of them approach the edge of the balcony and look out at nature. They breathe in the fresh air.

"You're right, this is awesome," Desdemona says. She kisses Kevin. Whenever she sees something pretty she is compelled to kiss somebody. She tries to kiss Rick, as well, but he steps back before she can get too close.

"I don't trust this balcony," Rick says. "If it collapses we're fucked."

"I'm sure it's fine," Jason says. "My grampy invested a lot of money into this place."

"When?" Rick says. "40 years ago?"

"Well, you better not be chicken shit about heights," Jason says. "Because this deck is where we're doing all of the partying."

"Hells yeah!" Kevin says. "Let's get the beer out of the car and start partying right now."

"Sounds like a plan," Jason says. "Why don't all of you unload the van while I figure out how to get the generator going."

"I'm on it," Kevin says.

They start drinking early. Rick and Des get drunk the fastest, drinking shots of vodka and mountain dew. Kevin and Crystal drink beers slowly while they get the barbeque going. Jason takes a while turning on the generator. He's not really sure how it works. He's also not sure why the water isn't working. After an hour or so, he gets the generator going but gives up on trying to figure out the water.

"You mean I'm going to have to shit outside?" Desdemona asks, her head on Rick's lap.

"Yep," Jason says. "And no showers for a few days, either."

"We might as well have just gone camping," Desdemona says.

Then she takes a shot of vodka.

Stephanie is in the upstairs bathroom crying again. She is brushing her teeth while crying. She needs somebody to talk to but she doesn't know who. She's really not that close with anyone. Crystal is the closest thing to her best friend but Steph is listed as sixth or seventh on Crystal's best friend list. Stephanie saw the list in Crystal's diary last year.

She looks in the mirror and pretends that her mirror image is a close enough friend to confide in. She tells the mirror image friend her problems. She tells it about how she's sleeping with her brother. Not because she wants to but because she's scared of what he will do to her if she refuses. She tells it about how he beats her and humiliates her, about how he makes her lick black ants off of his dick after school before their mom gets home. The ants bite her tongue as she sucks him. They bite his penis as well, but he says he likes the pain. He says that she should like it, too.

She brushes her teeth until her gums bleed, crying at herself in the mirror. Punching herself in the stomach until her bellybutton swells and bruises.

Jason takes Kevin aside out on the balcony.

"Hey, I've been thinking," Jason says in a whisper. "You should try to hook up with Stephanie this weekend."

"Stephanie?" Kevin asks.

"Yeah, she totally likes you, man," Jason says.

"But I'm with Des, man," Kevin says.

"Come on, Kevin. Desdemona is Rick's girl. Just because he lets you fuck her every once in awhile doesn't mean you're together. You need to finally find your own girl."

"Like Stephanie?"

"Yeah, dude," Jason says, strengthening his whisper. "She totally wants you. I promise. She keeps hiding out in the bathroom because you make her nervous. I see the way she looks at you. She totally wants it. You *have* to hook up with her."

"Whatever dude," Kevin says, laughing.

Kevin doesn't know what else to say. He just smokes his cigarette, shaking his head and laughing to himself about how clueless Jason is.

"I can't wait until we do it later," Desdemona says to Rick.

Rick ignores her. She kisses him on the neck.

"The infection's all cleared up now," she says. "We can do it all night."

Rick takes another shot of vodka as he holds in his stomach. The alcohol is causing stabbing pains in his guts and throbbing pains in his bones. Just barely eighteen and Rick already has ulcers. Rick's little sisters, who are only in middle school, also suffer from ulcers. It's a hereditary thing. Rick is usually fine to drink whatever alcohol he wants with his ulcers but never on an empty stomach. He's always hurting if he drinks alcohol, eats spicy food, or ingests anything with too much citric acid while he has an empty stomach.

"When the hell's dinner?" Rick cries, rubbing his belly and cringing at Des.

Desdemona can tell what's wrong with him. She shakes her head, thinking about how wimpy he is when it comes to pain. If he wasn't so sensitive about everything, she would make fun of him for being such a wimp. But she knows that would be a mistake. She knows he would pout about it for the rest of the night and probably withhold sex.

"Twenty minutes," Crystal says.

Crystal is sitting in a chair behind them. They didn't realize she had been there the whole time, listening to them. She is sticking labels on all of the food that is hers. She doesn't like other people touching her food. Everyone else is sharing the food, but she decided to divvy her share and put it in plastic bags with labels. If anyone touches her food she's going to freak. She can't handle eating anything that other people have touched. The labels have her name on them as well as pictures of kittens and puppies. She created the labels days ago.

"I need to eat," Rick moans.

"Twenty minutes," Crystal says, carefully sticking a label in the exact center of a plastic baggy filled with deviled eggs.

"Booyah!" Kevin says as he enters the living room with Jason.

Jason belches.

"You guys aren't done with that bottle *yet?*" Jason asks Rick and Des.

Desdemona sits up from the couch and picks up the bottle. 60% of the vodka is gone. "What do you mean, we've practically finished it?"

"It's still half full," Jason says. He grabs the bottle away from her. "I'll show you how a man drinks."

As Kevin digs two flashlights out of his backpack, Jason chugs the rest of the bottle of vodka and tosses it across the room. Then he blows the fumes rising from his throat into Desdemona's face. She wipes away the air like he had just farted at her.

"What's your problem?" Desdemona says.

"I'm just too damn awesome, that's what," Jason says.

Desdemona rolls her head against Rick's shoulder. She doesn't care that much about the vodka. She's already drunk. Rick writhes in pain next to her, but she pretends he's just cold and wraps her arms around him to make him warm.

Crystal gives her boyfriend a dirty look as she places her labeled food back into the cooler. "What the hell are you two up to?"

Kevin says, "We're going to explore," while flashing his flashlight in and out of his mouth.

"Where?" Crystal says.

"We're just going to see what's in the attic," Jason says.

"Now, just before dinner?" Crystal asks. "You're going to get your hands all dirty."

"We won't be long," Jason says.

"You're not trying to find your grandpa's guns are you?" Crystal says.

"Maybe . . ." Jason says.

"I don't want you messing with guns while you've been drinking," Crystal says. "Somebody's going to get shot in the face."

"No they won't," Jason says. "I know what I'm doing."

Jason and Kevin turn around and leave the room.

"Damn idiots," Crystal says, getting to her feet. "I better go after them and make sure they don't kill themselves." She steps around the couch to face Des, "You seen Stephanie?"

"Bathroom," Desdemona says.

"Shit," Crystal says. "Why don't you tell her the sausages will be ready in ten minutes."

"She doesn't eat sausages," Desdemona says. "She's vegetarian."

"Oh, fuck, I forgot."

"You didn't bring any tofu dogs?"

"No."

"Will she be able to eat anything?"

"Maybe a potato," Crystal says. "Or marshmallows . . ."

"She'll be fine," Desdemona says.

Crystal grabs her little pink flashlight from the kitchen counter and hurries down the hall to catch up with her boyfriend.

The attic contains half a dozen 16-pound bowling balls that are hanging by chains from the ceiling. They swing slowly from side-to-side. On the floor, between the hanging bowling balls, are two small sculptures of children made out of bowling pins. Each one has pins for arms and legs, a pin for a torso, and an upside-down pin for a head.

"Your grandpa was seriously weird, dude," Kevin says, bending down to examine one of the pin-boy sculptures.

With his index finger, Kevin draws a smiley face in

the dust on the pin-boy's pin-head. He presses his thumb in the center of the face to make a nose.

"Cute," Jason says.

Crystal comes up the ladder, but she doesn't enter the attic. She peeks her head up inside and frowns at the dust around her. She doesn't like to go into attics or basements because they always make her itchy. She doesn't like the feeling of dust from old junk touching her. Just the thought of it is making her itchy already.

Jason finds the gun cabinet right away. "Here it is."

He opens the case, but it's empty.

"What the fuck?" Jason says. "My grandpa should have tons of guns here, somewhere."

Jason's grandfather had a gun fetish. He wasn't a hunter, a survivalist, or an ex-soldier or anything like that. He just liked to collect them and shoot them off every once in awhile. Jason was hoping he would be able to shoot off the guns over the weekend. He's sure his grandpa wouldn't have sold all of them.

Jason goes through the drawers of the gun case and finds a variety of bullets. In the bottom drawer, he finds a revolver. A Smith and Wesson .44 magnum revolver. He picks it up over his head.

"Booyah!" Kevin says.

"You found one?" Crystal whines.

"Hells yeah," Jason says, holding the gun up like he's Charles Bronson. "There's only one, but this one is plenty."

"Leave that up here," Crystal says. "You can't use that while you're drinking."

"I won't," Jason says.

"Then leave it," Crystal says.

"I won't load it," Jason says.

"Then why are you taking the box of bullets?"

"I'm not going to put them in the gun tonight."

While they argue, Kevin finds something interesting in the corner of the attic. It is buried under boxes of clothes. He interrupts them. "Hey, what's that?"

Jason and Crystal stop arguing and move their eyes over to the corner of the room.

"Oh, snap," Jason says. "It's my brother's old Theremin."

"You have a brother?" Kevin asks.

"I used to," Jason says, as he goes to the corner of the attic to take all of the junk off of the Theremin. "I wonder if it still works."

"Stephanie plays the Theremin," Crystal says. "She's supposed to be really good. She plays classical music on it. I think she's even played with an orchestra before."

"What the fuck's a Theremin?" Kevin says.

"We should have her play it!" Jason says. "I used to love when my brother played the Theremin. It's such a funny instrument."

Jason wipes the dust off of the Theremin. He hands the box of bullets to Kevin, sticks the revolver in his pants, then picks up the Theremin and carries it down the ladder.

"This is going to be sweet," Jason says.

Stephanie doesn't show up for dinner.

"Did you tell her it was ready?" Crystal asks Des-

demona as they eat dinner outside on the deck. They are
eating potato salad and sausages on buns with mustard and
ketchup.

"Yeah," Desdemona says. "I told her four times in
the last half hour."

"I hope she's not going to be like this all weekend,"
Crystal says.

"She will," Desdemona says.

"She's fixing up the Theremin," Jason says.

"Why?" Crystal says.

"I told her to," Jason says.

"What?" Crystal says. "We've been waiting for
her."

"She said she's not hungry," Jason says.

"Why didn't you say so?"

"I don't know," Jason says.

Crystal realizes that Jason is really drunk now. He's
having a difficult time eating his sausage. His mouth is covered in mustard. Crystal ignores him eating because it gross-
es her out. She is easily grossed out when it comes to food.
She thinks it's gross how people eat food with their hands.
She never touches her food. When she eats, she always uses
a fork and knife. Even this sausage on a bun; she is cutting
it up and eating it like a steak.

Kevin, who has never eaten a bratwurst with Crystal
before, stares at her with amazement. He gives her a look as
if it's the weirdest thing he's ever seen. She sees him staring
at her plate and thinks he's staring at her breasts. He notices
that she thinks he is staring at her breasts and his eyes divert
to Jason.

"This place is fucking dope . . . man," Kevin says to
Jason. "I want my own cabin in the middle of nowhere."

49

"I think it's freaky as fuck," Rick says, his mouth filled with sausage. "We're out in the middle of nowhere. Some crazy killer could come in here and slaughter us all in our sleep and nobody would be able to stop them."

"Yeah, right," Desdemona says. "This place is like a hidden fortress. Nobody's going to find it. Even if somebody can see our lights from the distance it would take them forever to figure out how to get up here. We're difficult targets. People are lazy. Even crazed killers. You're far more likely to get butchered in your sleep while living in the city."

"Unless there's a crazed killer living out here in the woods . . ." Crystal says.

"I doubt there's a crazed killer out there," Desdemona says, pointing her sausage at Crystal. "If there was one in the area don't you think he would have moved into this abandoned cabin a long time ago?"

"Actually," Jason says, looking up from his food with glossy eyes. "There is."

"There is what?" Rick asks.

"A crazed killer in the woods," Jason says, losing his balance in his chair.

"Bullshit," Desdemona says.

"Bullshit?" Jason yells, standing up.

"Sit down," Crystal says to Jason. "You've had way to much to drink."

"I'm fine," Jason says, patting his girlfriend on the shoulder. "Fine. But, it's true. My dad used to tell me about it when I was a kid."

Crystal pulls him down into his chair. "You're too drunk to tell ghost stories."

"I'm fine," Jason tells her. He composes himself. "It's a true story. His name's Buddy."

"Buddy?" Desdemona asks. "You're trying to scare us with a story about Buddy the crazed killer? Give me a break."

"No," Jason says. "Not Buddy the crazed killer. His name is Buddy the Lobster Boy."

"I'm not listening to this," Desdemona says, fluffing her mohawk. "This is going to be the worst ghost story ever."

"It's *not* a story!" Jason says. He's serious all of a sudden. He pounds his fist on the table. "When I was a kid my dad used to tell me and my brother the story of Buddy the Lobster Boy. He was this deformed freak. You know, one of those lobster people who are born with their fingers molded together. Remember I told you there's a lot of inbreeding rednecks up here that create scary mutants? Well, Buddy is the scariest of them. Not only does he have lobster hands, but he also has one of those stillborn fetuses conjoined to his head. Only, it's not attached to the outside of his head, it is inside of his head. So he has dead baby arms and legs sticking out of the side of his skull. And out of the top of his head is a little dead baby head."

Kevin tries to hold in his laughter when he pictures a guy with a little head growing out of the top of his head. Jason hears the snicker and pauses. He stands up and walks to the cooler carefully. He takes out a beer and cracks it open.

"He lives in these very woods," Jason says. "He has been killing people for years, but nobody has been able to stop him. Some people have seen him and lived. My dad was one of those people. He only kills people who look at him and then scream. You see, he hates the fact that he's so ugly. If you see him and scream in horror it will make him so angry that he will go into a murderous rage and rip you

51

to pieces. So my dad always told me to never scream while I'm out in these woods, no matter what happens. He told me never to show fear. He always told me that if I ever screamed the lobster boy would kill me. I've never screamed since."

Desdemona laughs. "Wasn't this the plot of some really lame horror movie from the '80s?"

"It's not funny," Jason says. "Buddy the Lobster Boy killed my brother."

Kevin snickers. He's not sure if Jason is joking about that or not.

"When we used to come here as kids," Jason says. "Me and my older brother used to play hide and seek in the woods. One time, I was the one hiding. I hid in a really good spot where my brother could never find me. I waited for what seemed like hours. He couldn't find me. Eventually, I heard a loud scream. My brother's scream. Something made him cry out. That's the last I ever heard from my brother. They searched for months, but could never find his body. My parents figured he fell off the cliff and was taken away by the river. But I know that's not what happened. I know that on that day while playing hide and seek, my brother found something else instead of me. He found Buddy the Lobster Boy. And when he saw those dead fetus limbs dangling out of Buddy's head, my brother screamed. Then Buddy killed him and dragged his body away."

Jason takes a long drink from his beer.

"So let that be a warning to you," Jason says. "While you're staying here, no matter what happens, no matter what you see, never, ever scream."

Jason looks at them all with a serious face. Then Jason smiles and yells out, "Unless you're having *sex*!"

Rick and Kevin burst into laughter.

"Booyah!" Kevin cries. He stands up and gives Jason a high-five.

"I totally got you guys!" Jason says.

"No, you didn't," Desdemona says. "That was the lamest attempt at a ghost story I've ever heard."

Crystal looks at her boyfriend and shakes her head.

Jason stops laughing and sits down. He stares down at his fingers and realizes he's much drunker than he thought he was. He doesn't know why he decided to bring his brother into the story. He never talks about his brother. Normally, the story is about his dad when he was a kid and a childhood friend of his dad's, but he wanted the story to have more impact this time so he made it about himself and his brother instead.

The fucking Theremin put him on my mind, Jason thinks. *I never would have brought him into the story if I didn't find that Theremin.*

He crushes his half-full beer can and tosses it over the balcony into the black forest below.

Crystal finally convinces Stephanie to join the party. Stephanie doesn't really want to party, but she agrees to play the Theremin for them. She has always wanted to play her Theremin for her friends, but she always figured they would think it was nerdy. The jocks and the cheerleaders always make fun of the band kids. She doesn't want anyone to think she is a nerd.

In the center of the living room, Stephanie begins to play. She plays a solo rendition of Ave Maria on the Theremin. Her friends are gathered around her, on the mustard yellow couches and chairs. Rick and Kevin have never even heard of a Theremin before. They watch in drunken amazement as Stephanie plays. The haunting music is like an electronic violin flowing through the dimly lit room, as Stephanie's fingers wiggle in the air. Kevin can't believe that Theremins are played without touching any part of the instrument. He doesn't know how Stephanie is able to figure out which notes are which just by manipulating her hands in the air.

Stephanie pours her emotions into the song. It is a powerful moment for them. Desdemona finds the song both sad and eerie, even though she always thought of Ave Maria as more of a pretty song. Even Jason is speechless.

After a couple minutes, Stephanie begins to think of the time when her brother caressed her back while she was playing the Theremin. It was before they started having sex. She was confused and disturbed, but she didn't stop him from doing it. She just kept playing while he rubbed her shoulders, neck, and lower back. Stephanie's eyes tear. She tries to shake it off, but the tears keep flowing.

Jason's eyes are also beginning to tear. He is thinking about his brother. He is thinking about how good Stephanie is at playing the Theremin, and how his brother might have become just as good if he would have lived long enough. He could have been hanging out with them, playing a duet with Stephanie right now.

Halfway through the song, Stephanie's hands go limp. The song breaks into a static hum. She can't go on any longer.

"Hey!" Desdemona says. "What happened?"

Desdemona is too drunk to notice Steph's tears.

"I'm sorry," Stephanie says, rubbing her eyes.

Jason stares at her with widening eyes. He rubs his tears and clears his throat.

"Keep playing," Jason says.

Stephanie sniffles.

"I said," Jason stands up, "keep playing."

"I'm sorry," Stephanie cries. "I can't do it anymore."

"Come on," Jason says, his voice cracks. His face is turning red.

"Jason, she's had enough," Crystal says. "Let her be."

Jason charges over to Crystal and grabs her by the hands and holds them over the Theremin. "Keep fucking playing!"

The Theremin makes shrieking feedback noises as Jason struggles with Stephanie's hands.

"Jason!" Crystal says. "What the fuck are you doing?"

Jason squeezes her wrists as hard as he can. Stephanie whimpers. He pulls her close to him and whispers firmly into her ear, "I just want to hear you play for a little longer."

"Don't be a dick, dude," Kevin says.

"Just finish the *fucking* song, you *fucking* cunt," Jason whispers closely so that nobody else can hear but Stephanie.

Stephanie shoves Jason away and runs out of the room, crying.

"Why the heck did you have to go and do that for?" Desdemona says to Jason.

"What?" Jason says. "I liked her song and wanted her to keep playing. What's the big deal?"

"You didn't have to be such a dick about it," Rick says.

"You too, Rick?" Jason says. "Why are you all ganging up on me? She's the one who is fucking up our trip by crying all the time. She can't even finish playing a simple song."

Crystal and Desdemona get up and leave the room. Rick and Kevin follow them. Jason stays behind, staring at the mustard yellow furniture.

"Fuck you all then," Jason says.

He steps over to the Theremin and wiggles his fingers over it like Stephanie was doing. All that comes out of it are ugly electronic squeals.

CHAPTER THREE
RICK

Rick is sitting next to Kevin. He has a secret that he is dying to tell him.

"Why are you looking at me like that?" Kevin asks.

Rick smiles. He wants to tell him, but he has to wait until later that night.

Though he likes women, Rick is much more homosexual than bisexual. He didn't really know this about himself until after he started sleeping with Kevin. He likes masculinity. He likes muscles and strong personalities.

He hasn't told anyone, but Desdemona really isn't all that important to him anymore. If she were to leave him he would be perfectly happy with just Kevin for the rest of his life. Sometimes he wonders if it wouldn't be better without her. After she got a mohawk and all those tattoos, Rick really hasn't been all that attracted to her. She looks more like a guy, but not his kind of guy. If she gained fifty pounds of muscle and got a crew cut instead of a mohawk, then he would probably be much more attracted to her. Unfortunately, that's just not Des's style.

There is something living out in the woods. Something not quite human. It is sharpening its teeth on rocks and eating live frogs down by the stream. It sees lights in the distance. Lights in a place that is usually dark. There is something bad about these lights. Something evil. It has to make the lights go away. It has to make the evil, all evil, go away.

Desdemona is peeing out in the bushes nearby. She is still quite drunk and her knees wobble as she squats. Weeds tickle the bottoms of her thighs. She cringes, worried that the tickling sensations might be caused by black spiders crawling towards her crotch. She closes her eyes tight, hoping to be done soon, but she had so much to drink that she has a lot to pee out.

"I fucking hate nature," Desdemona says, completely pissed off that the toilets aren't working in the cabin.

She wishes she could pee off of the balcony like the guys were doing. That would be so much easier. She's heard they sell a device, a small plastic (or sometimes cardboard) funnel-thing, that girls can use to pee standing up. If she had one of those she would use it. She would love to stand next to the guys and pee off of the balcony with them.

There is a sound like cracking twigs under footsteps coming toward her. She stops peeing and looks around. The forest is quiet. There aren't anymore noises. She isn't sure if the footsteps were just her imagination. She couldn't really hear too well over the sound of her urine splashing against the ground.

There is another cracking of twigs. She can't tell

which direction it is coming from. The moon is bright enough
for her to see dozens of feet in every direction. There is no
movement. No prowlers in the dark. Frogs begin to croak
around her. Just a couple at first, then several. She can't see
them but she can definitely tell they are frogs. The croaking
makes it impossible to hear anymore footsteps.

She pulls up her pants and scurries back inside.

Next time I have to pee, she thinks, *I'm taking
Jason's gun.*

Kevin and Rick are making out in the living room
when Desdemona bursts in, rubbing her tattooed arms and
shivering. Rick looks kind of annoyed that she busted in on
them. His head is drunk and floppy.

"It's fucking cold out there," Desdemona says. "I
fucking hate pissing in the woods."

Kevin zips up his fly. "Wait until you have to shit."

"Fuck that," Desdemona says. "I'll wait and shit
when we get back home."

"Good luck," Kevin says.

Des opens a beer and takes a sip. It's warm and harsh
inside her mouth.

"Where's Crystal?" she asks.

"She said she was going to put Jason to bed," Rick
says.

"Is she coming back?"

"No," Rick says. "Jason said they were going to

have hot stinky sex."

"Stinky?" Kevin asks. "What is he going to take a dump on her or something?"

"A Cleveland Steamer?" Des says.

"A Hot Carl?" Kevin says.

"A Dirty Sanchez?" Rick says.

"Yeah, right," Desdemona says. "You know how easily grossed out Crystal gets. She wouldn't do anything like that in a million years. She probably has the most normal sex life of anyone you've ever met. And Jason, you know he only does missionary position. He probably doesn't even let her be on top."

"What a couple of pussies," Kevin says.

"Speaking of sex," Rick says, standing up off of the couch. "Are you two ready?"

"Hells yeah!" Kevin says.

"You're finally going to do it?" Desdemona asks Rick. "After all these months?"

"Yeah," he replies. "My doctor says it's okay to have sex now."

"I couldn't imagine having a urinary infection that lasted that long," Kevin says. "At least you didn't pass it on to us."

"That's why I kept my shorts on during sex," Rick says.

"It's about time you got it working again," Desdemona says. "You totally suck at trying to give me an orgasm with your tongue."

"Yeah, your tongue's pretty short, dude," Kevin says. "Des can get her tongue in my ass three times farther than you can."

Rick flicks the side of the Theremin as he walks

across the room.

"Let's go," Rick says in an annoyed tone.

He really hates being criticized and teased, even when it's by his closest friends who are just joking around and don't mean him any harm. He's kicked people's asses for much less.

Crystal and Jason are in the master bedroom. They take the sheets off of the bed and then make it with bedding that they brought with them. Crystal refuses to sleep on beds unless they have her bedding. She even brings her own sheets and blankets to Jason's house and remakes his bed whenever she spends the night.

"You ready to do it?" Jason asks Crystal, wobbling drunkenly over the bed in just his socks and whitey-tighty underwear.

"Not tonight," Crystal says, lying in bed with the covers up to her shoulders.

"Why not?" Jason slobbers.

"Because you're drunk," she says. "And you're a fucking asshole."

"What? What's wrong with you?"

"Just go to sleep," she says.

He crawls into bed with her.

"Come on," Jason whispers into her ear.

She doesn't reply.

"You know you want to," he says, trying to be seductive.

Crystal isn't interested. His bratwurst and onion breath against her face turns her off completely.

"I brought a surprise with me," he says. "Something that's going to blow you away."

Her eyes light up. She turns around.

"You mean . . ." she begins.

He nods.

"Serious?" she says.

He goes to his backpack and pulls out a stack of photographs. He looks down on them and licks his lips. Then he looks at Crystal and nods his head. Crystal raises her eyebrows at him and sits up.

"Fucking awesome," Crystal says.

Jason brings the photos to her and drops them in her lap. She spreads them out across the bed quickly. Her eyes go wild at all of the imagery.

"Ooooh, *yeah*," Crystal says, rolling her tongue in the air as she looks through them.

They take off their clothes and sit on opposite sides of the bed, examining the photographs. The pictures are of naked Asian women who are in the middle of getting abortions. When Crystal sees one of the half-aborted fetuses, she slides a clean glass baby arm-shaped dildo between her legs and bites her lower lip.

Crystal has a fetish for erotic abortions. It is a highly illegal and quickly growing phenomenon in the underground pornography world. The majority of it comes from some poverty-stricken region of Asia. Crystal heard about the fetish online. At first she thought it was gross and kind of funny, but then it started to turn her on.

Jason and Crystal don't really have sex very much. Sometimes, but not very often. Crystal doesn't like to have sex. She doesn't like fingers touching her vagina, not even her own fingers. Fingers disturb her for some reason. They gross her out. She doesn't like penises, either, because they remind her of giant swollen fingers. So her sex life with Jason mostly consists of masturbating together while looking at erotic images.

When she masturbates, Crystal always uses a dildo. She never uses her fingers. Her favorite dildos are made of glass or metal. She likes the cold hardness of glass and metal. Jason always asks her why her favorite dildo is shaped like a baby arm, and she always gives the same answer.

"There's fingers on it," Jason always says. "I thought you were disturbed by fingers?"

"I am," Crystal always says. "But they kind of turn me on, too."

Jason doesn't really understand Crystal. He doesn't understand why she is so easily disturbed by food and fingers, yet finds pictures of abortions sexually gratifying. He assumes she has some major issues.

A lot of the abortion porn involves sex. Sometimes there will be a guy forcing the woman to suck his dick while she is getting an abortion. Other times the aborted fetus parts will be used in some kind of depraved sexual acts by the people watching the abortion. The parts are usually sucked on or inserted vaginally. There have been rumors about a video where a woman inserts every piece of a freshly aborted fetus into her asshole and then shits it out onto another woman's breasts. Both Crystal and Jason hate this kind of thing. They think that the pornographers cross the line when they incorporate sex into the abortion. Crystal thinks it's not only in bad taste, but it also ruins the fantasy.

Crystal has never had an abortion, but she imagines it to be a sensual and erotic experience. The thought of having a living being grow inside of her and then having it removed drives her wild. While masturbating, she likes to imagine that she is the one receiving the abortions in the photos. And she likes to imagine that Jason is the fetus that is being aborted.

She likes to think that she has magic powers and could transform her boyfriend into a pool of cum while he masturbates. Then she fantasizes about how she would collect him into a turkey baster and then squirt him inside of her. He would become a part of her, develop into a fetus inside of her body. He would be consciously aware of this the entire time. Then, after weeks of growing in his girlfriend's womb, she would have him cut slowly out of her one piece at a time, or perhaps she'd have him vacuumed out of her quickly. She imagines that this act would be like having the biggest orgasm of her life. She imagines climaxing, squeezing her thighs around the surgical equipment, as some faceless doctor brutally murders her tiny boyfriend inside of her and then scoops him out in pieces. After his parts are thrown away, Crystal imagines she would move onto another boyfriend and start the process all over again.

She knows it's a cruel fantasy to have. She doesn't think of herself as a cruel person. There's just something deep inside of her that attracts her to these fantasies. She's worried that these feelings will make her a bad mother in the future. She's worried about what they mean.

Jason pretends like he is into this kind of pornography, but he's not really. He doesn't find it compelling nor disturbing. He doesn't really care. What turns him on is watching Crystal masturbate so excitedly. She is, without a doubt, the sexiest girl in school. Even though he doesn't get to have real sex with her very much, just masturbating while watching her touch herself is good enough for him.

Crystal's moans can be heard throughout the entire cabin as she masturbates. Desdemona and Kevin are in their room, listening to the moans through the air vent and giggling to each other.

"They sure sound like they're having fun," Kevin says.

"Yeah," Desdemona says, "with their boring missionary sex."

Rick is making a bed on the floor with their sleeping bags. He is nervous with anticipation. Adrenalin and alcohol are pumping through his system. He feels like his head is floating. He has been waiting for this night for a long time now.

Desdemona pulls off her top to reveal her tattooed breasts. The collage of pink, purple, and baby blue butterflies flutter across her chest and circle her nipples. Kevin pulls off her shorts and panties, as she pulls off his shirt and caresses his smooth head.

Rick hesitates taking off his clothing. His hand is shaking. He doesn't know how to break the news to them.

Stephanie is in the bathroom brushing her teeth. Again. She has lost all feeling in her mouth. Her gums are so bloody that her teeth have turned pink. There isn't any water in the sink, so she rinses out her mouth with warm, flat beer.

Something moves in the corner of her eye. Some kind of shadow casts over her for a brief moment. She turns and looks. It is gone now. It came from the bathroom window above the shower. Stephanie has no idea what it could be.

She steps onto the edge of the bathtub and looks out of the window. There is a pine tree next to the window. Some of the branches on the tree are rocking back and forth, but there isn't any wind. Something must have brushed by them. Something big, like an elk. She scans the dimly lit landscape for animals, but there is nothing there. She continues watching, brushing her teeth slowly, until the branches slow their swaying to a standstill.

"I have a confession to make," Rick tells Desdemona and Kevin.

Desdemona and Kevin are naked and kissing each other hard. The kind of kissing you only do when you're extremely drunk and horny. They pull themselves away from each other to hear Rick out. They don't understand why he hasn't taken his clothes off yet.

"I'm really sorry," Rick says, "but I've been lying to you both."

"Lying?" Kevin says. "About what?"

"I never had a urinary tract infection," Rick says. "I wanted it to be a surprise for you. That was just my cover story so that I wouldn't have to have sex with you while it healed."

"While what healed?" Desdemona asks.

Rick opens his mouth to speak, but nothing comes out. His face turns red and he smiles nervously. He decides to show them instead of tell them. He pulls down his pants.

Kevin and Desdemona can't really tell what he's trying to show them. They move in closer. Then it hits them and both of their mouths drop open.

"What the fuck?" Desdemona says.

"No fucking way," Kevin says. "You're fucking with us, right?"

Rick doesn't have a penis anymore.

"What happened?" Desdemona cries. "This isn't for real, is it?"

Rick spreads open the lips of his vagina to prove to them that it is real.

"It's a fucking vagina!" Kevin cries, laughing.

Rick suddenly feels embarrassed and ashamed.

"I had the operation on my birthday," Rick says. "It's beautiful, isn't it?"

"That's fucking insane, bra!" Kevin says.

"You mean you did this on purpose?" Desdemona says.

By the tone of Desdemona's voice, Rick can tell she doesn't approve. She steps away from him.

"You don't like it?" Rick asks her.

"What do you think?" Desdemona snaps. "I'm straight. Of course I don't like vagina."

"But it's my vagina," Rick says. "And you like me."

"I'm not a lesbian. I like guys. Why would I want you to have a sex change?"

"I didn't have a sex change," Rick says. "I'm still a guy. I just wanted to have a vagina instead of a penis."

"That makes you a girl," Desdemona says.

"But I'm not going to change anything else about me," he says. "I'll still be exactly like me. The sex will just be better."

"How will sex be better?" Desdemona asks. "It was perfect before. The dick-to-hole ratio was perfect. Now we're short one dick. What are we supposed to do, use a strap-on?"

"I bought a strap-on," Rick says.

Desdemona shakes her head. "This really sucks."

"I think it's pretty fucked up that he didn't tell us," Kevin says to Desdemona. "But, you know, there's no going back for him now. We might as well accept it and move on."

Desdemona looks down at her feet and grumbles. Rick approaches her.

"I'm sorry I didn't tell you about it," Rick says. "But this is what I really wanted. This is who I really am. Inside, I have always been a man with a vagina."

Desdemona snorts at him.

"Look," Rick says, opening his vagina to her. "Just give it a shot. I'm sure you'll grow to like it."

"I guess I'll give it a try," Desdemona says.

Rick claps his hands.

"Great!" he says. Then he lies down on his sleeping bag and spreads his legs, waiting to be fucked like a woman.

Desdemona and Kevin look at each other. Desdemona rolls her eyes. Kevin shrugs at Des and goes down on his hands and knees. He slides his penis into Rick's vagina and they both grunt.

"This is fucking ridiculous," Desdemona mutters, as she squats down into Rick's face so that he can give her oral sex.

From the bathroom, Stephanie can hear everyone else in the cabin having sex. Kevin's moaning is the loudest. Stephanie has had the biggest crush on Kevin ever since Freshman year. She closes her eyes and concentrates on Kevin's voice. A smile curls up on her lips. It's the only genuine smile to cross her face in months. Then the smile turns to a frown.

Stephanie hates Desdemona. She hates how Des has two boyfriends and she doesn't even have one. She thinks Des is a greedy bitch.

Kevin should be my boyfriend, Stephanie always thinks.

She hopes that someday Kevin will be her boyfriend. She hopes that he will marry her. Then he'll protect her from her brother. He'll take her away from her horrible family. He'll make sure nothing bad happens to her ever again. If it wasn't for Desdemona maybe Kevin would have already done these things for her. Maybe none of the crap she is going through right now ever would have happened.

Her eyes drift shut as she imagines Kevin making love to her. He moans with passion as he enters her. Stephanie unzips her pants and pulls them down to her ankles. She brushes her teeth with one hand as the other hand slides down into her thick bush of black pubic hair.

After she becomes moist, she opens up her vaginal lips to reach her rows of vaginal teeth. None of her friends know about this deformity. Stephanie was born with vagina dentata… she has teeth in her vagina. It is a very rare condition. Stephanie is one of only three women afflicted with the disease in the United States. Once she turns eighteen, she'll be able to have them removed. Until that time, she's stuck with them. Her mother has always refused to pay to get them removed. Her mother always says, *God made you that way for a reason.* And that's always the end of that discussion.

Stephanie takes the toothbrush from her mouth and brings it down to her vaginal teeth. She brushes these lower teeth very slowly and carefully. She becomes more lubricated and brushes faster, then faster. This is the only way Stephanie can have an orgasm.

She lets out a loud sigh from her raw, bloody mouth, listening to her future lover's moans, and brushing her vagina's teeth in pink foamy ecstasy.

Desdemona is making out with Kevin while they both ride on top of Rick. At first, she finds it sensuous to be able to focus on Kevin for a change. Rick is such a Leo that he always wants all the attention to be on him, so it usually seems like Des and Kevin are making love to Rick, rather than all three of them making love to each other. Desdemona kisses Kevin passionately, and he licks the green butterfly tattoos on her neck.

But Desdemona gets bored easily. Rick is horrible at giving oral sex. As Kevin had mentioned, he has a small tongue. It doesn't go very far out of his mouth. Not only is size a problem, but he has no idea how to control his tongue, or how to give a woman an orgasm.

Since she isn't getting pleasure sexually, Desdemona finds pleasure in squeezing her thighs around Rick's head and grinding her crotch into him as hard as she can, suffocating him. It helps her release all of the anger and frustration inside of her. But Rick gets annoyed and just stops licking her entirely. He pushes on her vagina with the bridge of his nose and holds it there as she straddles him.

After a few minutes of this, Desdemona gives up.

"Fuck this," she says, standing.

Rick takes a deep breath of air. His eyes are closed. He won't even look at Desdemona. He is too focused on his first experience with vaginal intercourse on the receiving end. She steps away from them and grabs her clothes.

"I'm going to go masturbate," she says, frustrated.

The guys don't even acknowledge her. They pull a sleeping bag over their heads and continue without her. She leaves the room and slams the door.

Desdemona stomps down the stairs and bursts into the bathroom. She catches Stephanie in the act of masturbating with her toothbrush.

"Oh, fuck!" Desdemona cries.

Stephanie shrieks and pulls the toothbrush out. She holds it up like a butcher knife. She doesn't know what else to do.

Desdemona closes the door and laughs. "Sorry about that."

Stephanie doesn't say anything. She's pissed off at Des for walking in on her like that. She wants her to die. Panic ripples through her forehead as she realizes Des might have just seen her vaginal teeth. She is worried that she might tell everyone. She is worried that everyone will think she's a freak.

Desdemona waits outside the door for a while. She did not see anything out of the ordinary. She just saw a girl with her pants down to her knees with some kind of object sticking out of her vagina. She didn't even realize it was a toothbrush. After thinking it over, Des decides to go back to her room to rejoin the sex…even if she just has to masturbate next to the guys.

When Desdemona returns to the bedroom, both of the guys are done having sex. The light is off. They are curled up together and drifting into sleep.

"Bitches!" she mutters to herself.

They didn't save any room for her under the covers, but she forces herself in anyway, behind Kevin. Kevin is breathing heavily and covered in sweat, as she wraps her arm around him. She feels Rick's ribs against the back of her hand and gently grinds her knuckles into them until he moves. Then she's able to slide her hand between the two of them, all the way around Kevin's body. She can probably pull Kevin on top of her and have him finish her off, but she decides to let it go. The sexual energy she had been feeling all day has vanished. She closes her eyes and tries to sleep. She tries to push the anger and dissatisfaction out of her mind.

They've got a rule that nobody goes to bed until everybody has an orgasm. This is the first time that rule has been broken. Since Desdemona left the room in a huff, she'll forgive them for it this time. But in the morning, she'll have her boyfriends make it up to her. Maybe she'll even give Rick oral sex and show him how it's supposed to be done.

Stephanie's room is on the ground floor. She doesn't want to be on the ground floor, because that's where all the big creepy bugs like to roam. She can't handle bugs. She decides to sleep on the living room couch in her sleeping bag, instead of on the floor in the room she was given. She would rather not sleep on the floor.

But she's not able to sleep anywhere. Too many thoughts are racing through her mind. She just reclines on the couch and stares at the ceiling.

A window shatters in the next room.

She leaps off of the couch and looks around. The noise came from the bedroom, the room she was supposed to be sleeping in. Jason's revolver is on the coffee table. Stephanie picks it up. It's not loaded. She searches the room for the box of bullets.

Nobody else seems to have heard the shattering sound. She wonders why they haven't heard it. She wonders if they were the ones who caused the noise. The bullets are on the kitchen counter. She frantically loads the revolver with three bullets and drops the other three. *Three's plenty,* she thinks, and leaves the other bullets on the floor.

The gun is pointed out in front of her as she enters the bedroom and turns on the light. The room is empty. The window is intact. She looks out of the window. In the moonlight, she can see all the way across the clearing. Nobody is out there. She lowers the gun and leaves the room.

She doesn't notice that the outside lamp has been smashed with a rock.

After that, Stephanie realizes that she's not going to get any sleep. Her toothbrush is dirty now, so she can't use it to brush her teeth, even though she's incredibly anxious. Normally, she keeps a toothbrush on her at all times for brushing, and another hidden in her room for masturbating. She wishes she would have brought that toothbrush with her.

Sitting on the couch with the gun in her lap, she sighs and stares blankly at the Theremin centering the room. Then she begins to cry.

She looks down at the gun in her lap and wonders if she has the guts to use it on herself. She's contemplated suicide before, dozens of times, but she's never been able to go through with it. She often tells her mother that she's contemplating suicide, as a way of asking for help. But her mother always smacks her across the face and says, *suicide is a one-way ticket to hell*. And that's always the end of that discussion.

Unfortunately, the only cure for her problems that she can think of at the moment is suicide. She doesn't want to kill herself but she feels trapped against a brick wall and doesn't know what else to do. She doesn't want to have the baby. It's her brother's. Stephanie's brother never used condoms when he forced her to have sex with him. He liked to *ride bareback*, as he called it. It was only a matter of time before she got knocked up.

She doesn't want to be a mother at her age, let alone the mother of an incest baby. As soon as she discovered she was pregnant, she decided to get an abortion. Unfortunately, since she isn't yet eighteen, the state-law says that she needs to get her mother's permission. But she didn't want to tell her mother about this. She didn't even dare tell her brother.

Telling her mother about the pregnancy was the worst thing she ever could have done. Stephanie's mom is a devout evangelical Christian and is completely opposed to abortion.

Her mother said, *this child doesn't belong to you, it belongs to God. If you have an abortion you aren't just murdering your child, you are murdering God's child.*

Not only is her mother forcing her to have the child, she is forcing her to raise the child with her brother as mother and father. *It's your responsibility*, her mother says. And she told Stephanie that if she does anything to stop this baby from being born that she would cut the uterus out of her so that she could never have another child ever again.

God's retribution, her mother calls it.

Stephanie's brother smiled when he found out that he had impregnated his sister. He seemed to like the idea of having that kind of control over her. He had no plans to actually help raise the kid, but he thought it was funny that his sister was going to be forced to have his baby.

You deserve it, he told her.

Her mother didn't care when she found out that Stephanie's brother was forcing her to have sex with him. She looked at Stephanie as if she didn't even hear what she had said. It didn't even seem to bother her. All that matters to Stephanie's mother is that the baby is born and not aborted. She will do everything in her power to make sure this comes true.

Stephanie caresses the barrel of the gun. She loves thinking about how her mother will react when she finds out that Stephanie has killed herself. There's nothing her mother can do to her then. Her mother will lose. Stephanie will win.

If only she had the guts to do it . . .

CHAPTER FOUR
JASON

Jason awakes to a loud bang. He lifts his head from his pillow and listens carefully, wondering where the noise came from. Everything is silent. He decides it was just something he heard in his dream and lays his head back down. He looks over at Crystal. She is dead asleep. She is lying on her side, near the edge of the bed, as far away from Jason as possible. She says she can't sleep if she can feel his body heat near her, so she always sleeps as far away from him as possible.

A hangover is already growing inside of Jason's head. He needs some aspirin and some water. He's not willing to leave the bed to get them. Memories flow into his mind and he smacks his forehead. He remembers the way he treated Stephanie when she was playing the Theremin. It's not that he feels bad for treating Stephanie in such a cruel manner, it's that he is worried that his friends will like him less for doing it. He could care less about Stephanie. He thinks she doesn't belong in their circle of friends and should be cast out. If he made her feel like she doesn't belong then that's great news for him. But if he ostracized himself in doing that then he's going to have to save his reputation somehow.

The Theremin made him a little emotional. It reminded him of how he lost his brother, all those years ago. Then that made him think about how he lost his mother in the car crash and how he lost his grandfather last year. Most of all, it made him realize that he's going to be all alone soon. His dad was recently diagnosed with Leukemia. He isn't sure how long he has to live, but the doctor says up to three years. Jason doesn't want to join the military next year, but his dad is making him. He's worried that his dad will die while he's away. He's worried that he won't have much time left with him.

You need to be a man, Jason's dad always says. *You don't need anybody in this life but yourself.*

Jason jumps out of the bed to the noise of a woman screaming.

"What's going on?" Crystal says as the screams drag her out of sleep.

Jason runs into the hallway wearing just his socks and his whitey-tighties. Crystal follows him in her pajamas. They go downstairs into the living room where the screams are coming from. It is Desdemona. She's in her pink bra and panties. Her face is dark red and her eyes are flooded with water, makeup running down her cheeks. Rick is holding her in his arms.

Crystal goes to Desdemona but stops before she reaches her. Something else has grabbed her attention.

She turns to her right and sees the body. Then she screams herself.

"Holy shit!" Crystal cries. "What the fuck?"

Stephanie's body is limp on the sofa, the barrel of the gun in her mouth. The wall behind her is covered in blood and chunks of meat. A large section of her skull is missing.

"Ohmygod, ohmygod, ohmygod!" Crystal cries, shaking her hands at the air.

"I can't fucking believe she did it," Rick says.

"What the fuck happened to her?" Desdemona says.

After a few moments of panic and then a few moments of silence, Crystal pushes Jason.

"This is all your fault," she says.

"Me?" Jason cries.

"You made her feel bad," Crystal says.

"No, it's my fault," Desdemona says. "I embarrassed her right before she did it. Big time. It wasn't that major of a thing, but I think it was the cherry on top that pushed her over the edge."

"It's none of your faults," Kevin says. "You all know why she did it."

Everyone pauses. They know she has abusive parents. Not physically, but mentally abusive. They also know about her brother. It now seems obvious to them that this kind of thing was bound to happen sooner or later. They wish they would have been better friends to her.

"What are we supposed to do?" Desdemona says.

"We have to call the police," Rick says.

"Fuck that," Jason says. "We've all been drinking. They're going to arrest us. Or, worse, they're going to blame us for her suicide. They might even think we killed her."

"Then what do you want us to do, bury her in the woods?" Rick says.

"Why the hell not?" Jason says.

Stephanie leaps off of the couch and screams out in agony. She grabs Jason by the arm and shakes globs of blood onto his bare chest.

"What the fuck!" Jason says.

He rips his arm out of her grip and she falls back onto the couch.

"She's not dead," Crystal cries, going to her friend's side.

Stephanie is hyperventilating and her body is jerking. She stares straight ahead but it doesn't look like she can see anything.

"What do we do?" Desdemona says.

"We need to get her to the fucking hospital," Crystal says. She turns to Jason. "You have to drive her there."

"I'm too fucked up," Jason says. "Call an ambulance."

"Our cell phones don't work up here!" Crystal says.

Kevin takes out his cell phone and double checks. "Yeah, there's absolutely no signal on this thing."

"We're going to have to get her there ourselves," Crystal says.

"I'm not that drunk," Kevin says. "I can probably drive."

"Let's get her into the van," Crystal says. "Quick."

Crystal and Rick carry Stephanie by her shoulders. Desdemona and Kevin hold her up by her feet. They can't see where they are going as they stumble drunkenly through the woods, trying their hardest not to drop the wounded girl.

"How the hell is she still alive?" Kevin says. "The back of her fucking head is gone."

"People survive shots to the head all the time," Desdemona says. "Even people who put shotguns in their mouths survive from time to time, even when their face has been blown off."

"If she survives," Kevin says, "she's probably going to be brain damaged."

"Let's just focus on her survival right now, okay?" Crystal says.

They place her carefully into the backseat of the van, on top of empty beer cans and candy wrappers. Pork rind crumbles stick to the open wound on the back of her head. Crystal brings her hand to the brainy mess to brush away the crumbs, but stops short, worried that she might get the blood or greasy food on her hand. She decides to let the doctor handle it, even if the pork rinds get rubbed into her head during the drive down the mountain. Stephanie wheezes and spits mouth foam as they close the door on her.

"We'll be back soon," Crystal tells the others.

"What about me?" Desdemona says. "I want to go, too."

"Stay here," she says. "You're all too fucking drunk."

Rick pulls Desdemona back. "Let's stay." But De

breaks out of his grip.

Kevin pulls out the keys and rushes to the drivers side door, then notices something on the ground.

"Oh, fuck," he says. "How the hell did this happen?"

"What?" Jason says.

The van has a flat tire.

"Must have ran over a nail or something on the way up here," Jason says.

"You've got to be shitting me," Crystal says.

"We've got to change it," Kevin says.

"There's no time," Crystal says. "Just drive on it."

"We'll never get down the mountain with this flat," Kevin says. "It'll be way too dangerous along that cliff."

"We're going to have to try," Crystal says. "All we need to do is get down the mountain far enough to use our cell phones."

Kevin doesn't argue. He gets into the van and starts it up. Rick, Jason, and Des stand there, watching as the van backs slowly down the hill. They wait there until it is out of their sight.

"There's no way she's going to make it through the night," Jason says.

Desdemona furiously rolls her eyes at him and walks away.

"Give it a rest," Rick tells Jason.

Something is watching them from the bushes as they walk through the woods back to the cabin. It sees Desdemona in her pink underwear, Rick in his sweat pants and t-shirt, Jason in his whitey-tighties and muddy gym socks. It creeps in closer to them, following them, listening to them argue.

"If she dies you're going to feel like such a dick," Desdemona tells Jason.

"I don't care if I'm a dick," Jason says.

"Don't you think of anyone but yourself?" she says.

"That's not how I was raised," Jason says.

"Then how were you raised?"

"To be a man," he says. "With no fear and no attachments."

"I have to pee," Desdemona says.

"Cool," Jason says, flipping her off.

Desdemona pulls down her pink panties as she squats. The others keep walking.

"Hey, aren't you going to wait for me?" Desdemona says.

"No, thanks," Jason says. Jason is the kind of guy who prefers to pretend that girls never actually go to the bathroom.

"Rick!" Desdemona cries.

Rick groans and turns around. He walks back to her and waits for her to pee. Jason goes back to the cabin by himself and cracks open another beer.

While she's peeing, Desdemona says, "We're never going to forget this night for the rest of our lives."

While he watches her pee, Rick says, "Yeah."

Desdemona thinks about how Rick has to pee sitting down from now on. However, she kind of remembers him peeing off of the balcony early that night. She wonders if he has one of those funnel things that make it possible for girls to pee standing up.

"Des," Rick says. "You know . . . I don't think we should be together anymore."

A wave of diarrhea hits Desdemona while in the middle of peeing. She tries to hold it in after hearing what Rick just said, but it splashes out of her without her control.

"I've been falling out of love with you for a long time now," he says. "With your tattoos and your mohawk. You're just not the Desdemona I used to know. Something's happened to you."

"You're breaking up with me *now*?" Desdemona says. "After what happened to Stephanie? While I'm in the middle of taking a dump?"

He didn't realize she was shitting. He just heard splashing noises and thought she was only peeing. His nostrils cringe at her.

"You're dumping me while I'm taking a dump?" She almost wants to laugh at that, but she's not in the mood.

Stepping back to avoid the smell, he says, "After how you reacted to my operation I realized that you're not somebody I want to be with anymore. I think I just want to be alone with Kevin for awhile."

"Does Kevin know about this?" she asks. "Is he dumping me, too?"

"I haven't talked to him, yet," he says.

"You can't dump me without getting his approval. This is a threesome relationship. He's my boyfriend just as much as he is yours. How do you know he doesn't want to stay with me and get rid of you?"

"Because I've been together with him longer than you," he says.

"Not really," she says. "You were only friends with him for longer. If you remember correctly I was his lover before you were."

"He loves me more than he loves you," Rick says.

"He doesn't love you more," Desdemona says. "He's not even gay."

Rick gasps like she had just knocked the wind out of him.

"He's not attracted to you," she says. "He never wanted to be dragged into this relationship with you in the first place. The only reason he started sleeping with you is because he was afraid of losing you as a friend."

By the way he glares at her, Desdemona realizes that what she just said upset him more strongly than she thought it would. Perhaps because he knows there's some truth to that. Perhaps he's known for a long time now.

"Fuck you, Des," he says. "It's over."

Then he turns around and walks away. Desdemona stands up to chase after him but another wave of diarrhea hits her and she is forced to squat down and continue. She winces as she feels her liquid shit running downhill and collecting against her bare foot.

"Ewww, *gross*," she says. "I'm never shitting in the woods again."

Desdemona realizes she is alone in the middle of the woods, barefoot, shit in her toes, her underwear around her knees, and she can't stop going to the bathroom. The cabin is an acre or two away. She can see a few of the cabin's lights up ahead, but she can't see much of the cabin. It is silent around her. There isn't even a breeze.

A rustling sound approaches her. It is the sound of an animal running through the bushes. She turns around. There is nothing there. She grabs some leaves from the ground and wipes her ass, but most of the leaves are mixed with dried pine needles that pierce and scratch her skin raw. She tries again, but she can't wipe it properly without toilet paper.

Something charges out of the bushes and runs past her. She doesn't know what it is. All she can see is movement. A gray blur. It rushes through the trees toward the cabin.

Desdemona quickly wipes her ass with her hand and rubs it against the bark of a nearby tree. She pulls her underwear up and crawls slowly forward, trying not to make a sound. It was something big and something fast. Either a deer or a really fast human.

After a few minutes of examining the distance, and seeing nothing, Desdemona decides that it must have been a deer. She straightens herself up, getting ready to head back. Then she realizes that she's extremely dirty and smells like shit, yet she won't be able to take a shower any time soon. She'll have to use bottled water. She groans when she remembers that all of the water is still in the van. She's going to have to clean herself off with beer.

A shattering sound forces Desdemona to drop back down on the ground. One of the lights at the cabin has disappeared. She crawls forward to get a closer look. She sees a rock fly out from the forest and smash into another one of the lights. It explodes into sparks and then becomes dark.

As the last of the lights is shattered, darkening the woods around her, she curses Rick for leaving her in the woods, and curses Crystal for not letting her go to the hospital with them, and curses herself for agreeing to go on this stupid trip in the first place.

Jason and Rick are out on the deck, drinking beers, smoking cigarettes, and looking up at the stars.

Rick doesn't feel much like drinking anymore. He uses his half-filled can of beer as an ashtray.

"My brother really did die out here," Jason says. "I wasn't making that part up."

Rick squints his eyes and looks over at his friend.

"We don't know how it happened," Jason says. "He just disappeared."

Rick puts out his cigarette into the beer can.

"I always figured my dad did it," he says. "The old asshole liked to shoot guns randomly into the woods back then. My grandpa always told him to use the targets, but my dad didn't care where the bullets went. He wasn't afraid of hitting anybody."

"You think he shot him?" Rick says.

"By accident," Jason says. "He probably hit him and killed him without knowing it. Once he found the body, I'm sure he buried it or figured out a way to get rid of it."

"But if it was an accident, why would he hide the body?"

"He would hide the body especially if it was an accident," Jason says. "He never lets anyone know when he makes a mistake, no matter what the cost. That's the kind of person he is."

"Fuck . . ." Rick says.

"Yeah . . . *fuck* is right," Jason says.

Rick sees something moving over Jason's shoulder, in the distance. He cuts Jason off and points at it. Jason turns and squints his eyes. There is a white figure crawling down the side of the cliff about eighty feet away from the side of the cabin.

"What the fuck is that?" Rick says.

"I can't tell," Jason says.

They watch as the figure moves like a spider climbing down a wall.

"It's like a monkey of some kind," Jason says.

"It looks like a man," Rick says.

"It can't be human," Jason says. "Nobody can climb a cliff like that. And it's too fucking fast."

"What the fuck do you think it is?"

Jason squints his eyes. "Some kind of alien." Then

he laughs at the idea.

Rick laughs with him and drinks a sip of his beer full of cigarette ashes.

The thing stops and looks at them with cold glowing eyes. They stop laughing. They realize this thing isn't a joke. It is real. And it is the scariest fucking thing they have ever seen. As they stand in a frozen stare, the thing climbs back up the cliff and disappears into the forest in front of the cabin.

"Shit," Jason says. "It's in our front yard now."

"Where's Desdemona?" Rick says.

"Probably downstairs," Jason says.

"She might still be outside," Rick says, running inside of the house and down the stairs.

Jason grabs the pistol as they run through the living room and out the front door.

"Des!" Rick calls to the dark woods. "Desdemona!"

"Desdemona!" Jason screams.

A white figure flies past them through the trees. They aren't sure if it is the thing from the cliff or not. They only see it for a second. Jason points the revolver at the figure and shoots twice. Both bullets miss.

"Des!" Rick calls.

The white figure turns around and darts towards them. It is definitely the thing from the cliff and it is a lot bigger than they thought it was. Jason points the gun and pulls the trigger, but it only clicks. He's out of bullets.

"Back inside!" Jason yells, as the figure gets closer.

Rick and Jason jump into the house and shut the door. The thing outside sweeps in at them and crashes into the side of the house. It scrapes on the screen of the door with what sounds like hooks or long fingernails.

"What the fuck is it?" Rick cries.

The thing turns the doorknob. Jason locks it. The thing breaks the doorknob off on the other side. It makes gurgling whisper sounds.

"It's a creature of some kind," Jason says.

"It looked like a really pale-skinned naked bald guy," Rick says.

"He's not fucking human," Jason says. "Did you see how fast he was running? Did you see him climbing that cliff? He's like a fucking vampire."

A loud pounding hits the door. The wood cracks. The creature slams its head into the door again, the wood cracks wider. Jason runs to the kitchen counter and reloads his revolver. He fires two shots into the door. The pounding stops. They hear the thing rush into the woods from where it came.

Jason loads two more bullets into the gun, to replace the ones he fired.

"Did I get it?" he asks.

"I don't think so," Rick says. "Might have wounded it."

They calm themselves and take some deep breaths. Jason opens another beer.

"That thing is for real, isn't it?" Jason says.

"It's real," Rick says. He throws Jason a shirt from his backpack so that his friend doesn't have to run around in his tighty-whitey's anymore, but Jason just tosses it aside. He doesn't need any clothes.

"Is it Buddy the Lobster Boy, in the flesh?" Rick asks, trying to make some kind of joke.

Neither of them think it is funny.

"It's not Buddy," Jason says. "Buddy was just a story my dad made up. This fucker is something real."

Rick nods. Then changes the subject. "I fucking hope Desdemona went upstairs to bed and isn't out there."

"If she's out there I'm sure she's dead by now," Jason says. "You shouldn't have left her."

"She pissed me off," Rick says. "How was I supposed to know this would happen?"

"Let's see if she's upstairs," Jason says. "Maybe we'll be lucky and find her asleep with her headphones on."

Desdemona is hiding in the woods, creeping towards the cabin one tree at a time. She heard the gunshots and the yelling. She saw the whole thing. But she was too afraid to reveal her position. She was too far away to reach them in time before they ran back into the house. She didn't get a good look at the thing that chased after them. It was just a gray figure.

Something rushes past her as she leans against a tree to blend in with the shadows. The thing darts through the woods right past Des, heading back towards the dirt road where the van used to be parked. She gets a quick look at the thing's back. He is a tall lanky man, completely naked, wiry with muscle, no body hair, light gray skin, and a hard, flat ass.

Desdemona doesn't know how long she will have this opening. She steps out of the shadows and runs for the cabin door. She charges into the clearing, cutting her bare heels on rocks and pine cones. A rustling noise whips past her and her vision becomes blurred.

The gray man moves like wind, passing her from behind, and then stopping in her path. Desdemona falls backwards, standing face-to-face with the thing. The creature is a man, but he is severely deformed. His eyes are low on his face with pupils that are dilated to the size of quarters. His mouth is filled with six small pointed teeth. On his head, he has two baby arms growing out like horns. Below his ears, he has baby legs growing out like sideburns snuggling against his cheeks. And on top of his head, there is a tiny baby head, staring squishy-faced at her. The limbs writhe and stretch against his skull like medusa's snake hair. The tiny baby head cocks at the girl as she stares at it.

Desdemona realizes that this thing is the creature from the ghost story Jason told at dinnertime. It wasn't just a stupid story. It was real. In the story, Jason said that this creature will only kill you if you scream. Des clenches her jaw. She will not scream.

The creature approaches her. It seems to be dazzled by Desdemona's tattoos and mohawk. It probably has never seen these things before. Des tries not to scream, tries not to even whisper, as the gray man sniffs the butterfly art on her skin.

She looks down and sees the man's hand. His fingers have been molded together, so each hand has a thumb and a fat bubbly mass of fingers.

The lobster boy brings his claw up to Desdemona's bare tattooed stomach. On his deformed fingers, there are curved metal blades. They look like metal crab claws. He has attached metal claws to his lobster hands so they can be used like real claws.

The claw cuts into Desdemona's belly and opens up her insides. Shock hits her before the pain. As she watches her guts spill out of her belly, she wonders, *why did he do it?* I didn't scream. *He wasn't supposed to kill me if I didn't scream . . .*

A voice in her head tells her, *but that was just a story . . .*

She screams in the gray man's face, causing him to recoil. She turns around and runs for the cabin, crying out for help, her intestines unraveling out of her as she runs.

Rick and Jason hear Desdemona's cries from upstairs. They quickly run down to the front door, and try to open it. But the door won't open.

"What's wrong?" Rick asks.

"I can't get it open," Jason says. "The thing broke the doorknob."

"Desdemona, we're coming," Rick yells.

He hears her crying his name on the other side of the door.

Jason kicks the door with the bottom of his foot. It still won't budge. He backs up as far as he can, then uses a football maneuver. He charges shoulder first and tackles the door off of its hinges, falling face-first down the steps into the dirt.

Rick looks outside to see the massive gray creature with a living fetus growing out of his head. Desdemona is on the ground below the freak. She is being pulled closer to the mutant by a dark slimy rope attached her midsection. It takes Rick a moment to realize that it is not a rope, but a vine of her intestine. The gray man whisper-gurgles at them and wiggles the baby arms on his head, as he tries to drag Desdemona into the woods by her own entrails.

Jason gets up from the ground and rushes forward. He shoots the revolver three times at the creature. Two of the bullets hit it square in the chest. It falls backwards onto the ground. It goes limp. Rick picks Desdemona off of the ground and helps her coil up her loose intestines like spaghetti and put them back inside of her.

"We need to get you to a hospital," Rick says.

She grows faint in his arms.

He takes her inside the cabin. Jason stays behind.

"Come on, Jason," Rick says. "I need your help."

Jason puts another bullet in the creature's head.

"What are you doing?" Rick yells.

"Just making sure," Jason says.

"Forget it," Rick says. "The thing is dead."

Jason runs back into the cabin and gets a good look at Des's open wound. "What can we do?"

"We can at least make her more comfortable and help her with the pain," Rick says.

"There's not that much pain, actually," Desdemona says.

"You're in shock," Rick says.

Jason doesn't realize the gray-skinned creature is getting up from the ground, wiping the stream of blood from its forehead to get a better view of his enemy.

By the time Jason notices the thing darting towards him, he doesn't have time to get the door closed. He fires the rest of his bullets at it, but only one of them connects. The creature doesn't go down this time.

"Upstairs!" Jason says, grabbing the box of bullets on his way up.

They go up to the second floor and out onto the deck. They close the arcadia door and watch for the thing. It should be right behind them.

"You shot it in the head," Rick says. "Why didn't it die?"

"Maybe the baby head's brain controls the body?" Desdemona says. "Maybe you have to shoot that brain?"

Jason hides behind the barbeque to reload his gun. He thinks that if the thing attacks before he finishes loading, it will go after Rick or Des first, buying him enough time to load the gun completely.

Desdemona sits down. She holds her spool of entrails tight to her body like she's hugging a pillow.

"I'll survive won't I?" Desdemona asks Rick. "Even though these fell out of my body, they can put them back in, right? Sometimes they cut miles of this stuff out of people and they live, don't they? Maybe they can't eat the same food as they used to, but they still survive . . . right, Rick?"

Rick nods at her but he doesn't look at her. He is busy watching the arcadia door, waiting for the thing to come towards it.

"Where is it?" Jason says, his hands shaking, dropping bullets everywhere.

He hits himself in the head for shaking so much. He shouldn't be shaking. He's not allowed to fear. His father would disapprove.

Rick says, "It's nowhere. It didn't come after us."

"Did it follow you upstairs?" Jason asks.

"I'm sure it did," Rick says.

Rick looks up and sees the gray man crawling like a spider along the side of the cabin. He is climbing with the metal claws on his hands and feet.

"It's up there," Rick cries.

The thing looks down at them and jumps onto the balcony. He goes for Rick first, lunging at him blades-first. Rick dodges with his football reflexes. The creature turns to Desdemona. She screeches and runs to the back of the deck, but it charges at her like a hurricane. It seizes her in its claws and then bites down on the center of her neck. Blood splashes into Desdemona's esophagus as the thing tries to rip her throat out with its teeth.

Rick runs at the creature like it's a football and kicks

it in the back of the leg as hard as he can. The creature wobbles but it doesn't loosen its grip. Rick punches it in the kidneys, in the spine, in the ribcage, but the thing won't budge. Desdemona's cries fill his ears. He can hear her blood gurgling in her throat as she screams in agony.

"I'm sorry, Des," Rick says. "I didn't mean to break up with you. I love you."

He tries desperately to pull the thing off of her, but he's not strong enough. Des grabs Rick by the hand, stopping him from struggling. She holds his hand tightly and rubs one of his fingers with her thumb.

I love you, too, Desdemona says with her eyes. Her lungs are filled with too much blood to say the words out loud.

Jason finishes loading his revolver. He steps out from behind the barbeque and fires wildly at the gray man. He doesn't bother to aim. He doesn't care who the bullets hit, as long as they kill the creature. He just pulls the trigger until there aren't any bullets left.

Two of the bullets miss the creature, two of the bullets hit the creature in the chest, one of the bullets hits Rick in the side of his belly, and the last bullet blasts the tiny fetus head into a messy pulp.

The gray man thrashes his arms wildly after his conjoined twin is decapitated. He slams himself through the railing of the balcony, and falls over the side, taking Rick and Desdemona with him. Jason runs over to the edge, but he doesn't see anything down there. Just a cracking of branches as the bodies hit the trees below.

It smells like sour shit inside the cabin as Jason steps in from the balcony. On the carpeting, Desdemona's brown footprints trail across the room. He rubs the smell out of his nose and goes downstairs to the living room, puts on his tennis shoes, and repositions his penis within his whitey-tighties. He reloads his revolver and puts the rest of the bullets into a fanny pack that he wraps around his waist. He's only got nine bullets left. He prays he doesn't need any more of them. He opens a bottle of Johnny Walker Red that he planned to save for the last night and takes a swig. It burns nicely. Then he exits the cabin and enters the woods.

Jason is going to prove to his father and to himself that he isn't afraid of anything. He is going to climb down the cliff and make sure that creature is dead. If it somehow survived, he's going to find another way to kill it.

He's not sure if Crystal and Kevin are going to make it to the hospital in time to save Stephanie or not, but he hopes they stay there for the rest of the night. He's not sure if he'll be able to save them if they come back too early.

CHAPTER FIVE
CRYSTAL

Crystal is outside of the van, guiding Kevin down the hill towards the cliff. They can't see very well in the dark, so they are going one inch at a time, trying to do it as safely as possible. It has taken them a long time just getting as far as they have. The flat tire doesn't move very well on the rough terrain. Kevin offered to hike down the hill by himself to call for help, because he thinks that would be quicker, but Crystal believes it'll be easier for the paramedics if they can get Stephanie as close to the highway as possible.

The edge of the cliff is not clearly visible. The van's headlights are so blinding and casting so many shadows, that Crystal is finding it difficult to approximate the distance they have before the path ends at a drop-off. Just moments before, the full moon was bright enough for them to see perfectly, but just when they needed the extra light clouds moved in and blocked out the moon.

"Keep going," Crystal says.

Kevin follows her directions, rolling down the hill and hitting the break every few inches.

Stephanie moans loudly from inside the van. She's beginning to regain consciousness and babbling in an alien

105

language. Crystal tries to block the moans from her thoughts. It's going to be twice as difficult if Steph wakes up and they have to keep her calm all they way down the mountain. But, then again, she might live longer if she's awake.

Crystal knows that Stephanie is pregnant. She spotted the signs earlier in the week. She could tell by the way Stephanie's been acting and the way she's been feeling. She knew Steph wasn't sleeping with anyone, so she doesn't know who the father is. She was worried that it might be Jason. The way he always shunned her, it seemed like Jason didn't want Stephanie around because he felt guilty about something. He wasn't the faithful type. And the way Steph was always the first person to arrive at Jason's house whenever he threw a party, it was as if she had a crush on him. But now, after all that has happened, Crystal is starting to put the pieces together. She is beginning to suspect that it wasn't Jason who impregnated Stephanie, but somebody closer to home.

She hasn't told anybody about it yet, but Crystal is also pregnant. Her plan was to tell Jason about it later on in the weekend, but she might just wait until next week when they're back home. She got pregnant on purpose. After she masturbated with Jason one time, while he was in the bathroom, she collected his sperm from the paper towel he masturbated into and put it inside of her with a long cotton swab. Of course, Crystal has no plans of having a child. She wanted to get pregnant so that she could finally fulfill her ultimate sexual fantasy. She wants to have an abortion.

It would have been perfect. She would have told Jason all about it and then they would have masturbated together, imagining how wonderful it's going to be to abort their own baby for real. She's never done this before because she was always worried that the process would turn out to be not as sensual and erotic as she imagined, that her fantasy would be ruined by reality, but she had become so obsessed with this fetish that she can't wait any longer. She has to try it out for real.

As she waves Kevin closer to the edge of the cliff, Crystal feels her belly and tries to imagine the size of the creature inside of her. She can't feel anything yet. It's still too small. She can't wait until it grows bigger. She wants to wait until the last possible moment before getting an abortion, so that it will be as developed as possible. She wants to be able to sense another being inside of her before it happens.

She is too busy feeling herself to notice Stephanie sitting up from the backseat behind Kevin.

Jason walks through the woods, holding his gun like an ice-cream cone. He is following the cliff, looking for a way down. The wind chills his bare back. Now that the moon is covered by clouds, he can hardly see a thing in front of him. He's beginning to wish he would have been better prepared for this excursion into the forest. He wishes he had brought a coat and a flashlight.

He tells himself, *don't be afraid of the dark. A flashlight only attracts the enemy. The cold keeps you alert.*

Tricking himself into believing this only helps a little. He can't help but feel crippled by the dark and the cold.

Once the lights of the cabin are completely out of his view and the darkness is at its thickest, he finds his way down: a rope ladder. He touches it to make sure he's not mistaking the ropes for something else in the shadows. It's real. He smiles. He was hoping that it would still be there. When he was younger, his dad and uncle hooked up this rope ladder so that they could get down to the river in five minutes rather than taking the forty minute hike down the hill. Jason's mother never let him or his brother use the ladder because she thought it was too dangerous, so this is his first time giving it a shot. It is also the first time anyone has ever tried to climb it in the dark.

The ladder is tied to a large tree. Jason pulls hard on the ropes to make sure they are still sturdy. He's not sure if the ladder has been used at all since he was a kid. He pulls again, this time putting all of his weight on the ropes. It seems fine. As strong as ever.

Peering off the edge and taking deep breaths, he tells himself *no fear, no fear*, over and over again. It is a lot darker and a lot farther down than he thought it was going to be. He puts his gun into his fanny pack and zips it up. Then he gets down on his hands and knees. He holds onto a rope with both hands and leans his legs over the cliff until they catch onto a rung. Then he lowers his weight onto his feet. He doesn't look down as he descends the ladder. He just focuses on each rung, taking them one at a time, pretending that it's no big deal.

I'm just as good as you, he says in his head. *I'm just as fearless as you.*

Living completely without fear is the most important lesson that Jason's dad wants to teach him before he dies. He thinks Jason must be fearless in order to succeed in this world. After high school, he wants Jason to join the military. Not because he thinks the military is the best thing for him, but because he knows Jason is afraid of joining the military. Jason is afraid he might have to go fight a war for a cause he could care less about.

It's like the time his dad called the cops on him for stealing and crashing the neighbor's car when he was fourteen years old, getting him put in Juvenile Hall for 30 days. He did this because he overheard Jason and a friend talking about prison life while watching an episode of OZ on HBO. Jason didn't even tell his friend that he was scared of the idea; he just said that he couldn't handle going to prison. This was enough for Jason's dad to think his son was too soft and needed to be toughened up.

It wasn't until two years later that Jason's dad told him that he was actually the one who stole the neighbor's car and that he did it to teach him a lesson. Jason was pissed at the time and wouldn't speak to his dad for weeks after that, but he eventually forgave him. Looking back on it, Jason is happy to have had the experience. It had made him a stronger person, even though he fell far behind in school because of it.

Jason thinks of nothing but his father as he climbs dozens of feet down the ladder. Once he is at level with the tops of the trees, he realizes that the rope doesn't reach all the way to the ground. He climbs as far down as he can until he gets to the end of the rope, but he's still about twenty feet off of the ground.

It is a consolation to him that the clouds are moving away from the moon, so at least he has some of his sight back. He looks down and sees the rest of the rope in the dirt. It must have broke a long time ago, while somebody else was climbing down. He wonders how long ago the ladder snapped. Probably years ago. If the rope was weak enough to break so long ago, he wonders why it is able to hold him up now. He wonders if he should jump down from here or climb back up. He's not sure which would be safer. If the rope is weak he would be better dropping twenty feet now, rather than falling forty or sixty feet if the rope breaks on his climb back up. If he was just a few more feet to his right he probably could climb down the side of the cliff. He wonders if he could jump for the cliff face and try to catch a handhold, but decides he would likely just rip himself to pieces against the rocks on the fall down.

Before he gets a chance to make up his mind, the rung holding up his feet snaps and he falls backwards, thrashing his limbs in the air as he tumbles. He looks down and tries to aim his fall so that he can land on his feet, but it's too dark to see the ground clearly.

Stephanie wraps her arms around Kevin's neck and slides her hands down his shirt. Kevin doesn't know what's going on as the bloody girl kisses him on the neck and whispers "I want you" into his ear like a drunken college slut with a busted tongue.

"What the hell?" Kevin yells.
He looks back at Stephanie. Her head is rolling from side-to-side. Her eyes flickering. She doesn't seem completely conscious.

She slithers her tongue down his neck towards his chest and rubs her open wound against the side of his face. He winces and tries to push her off of him.

"I've always wanted you," she says as she attempts to crawl over the seat to get to him.

Crystal yells at him from outside, asking him what the heck is happening, as the van gets closer to the edge of the cliff.

Stephanie pulls Kevin's penis out of his pants as he struggles to return her to the backseat. She rolls into his lap and drops all of her weight onto his right leg, forcing him to slam on the gas.

Crystal jumps out of the way as the van roars down the hill. Kevin slams on the breaks and lifts Stephanie's weight with all of his strength to get his foot off of the gas, but it's too late. The van's front wheels go over the edge and by the time the van comes to a stop, they are already hanging halfway off of the cliff.

The delirious girl puts his penis into her mouth and begins to give him a blowjob, as Kevin puts the van in reverse and tries to go back up the hill. The front wheels spin in midair. The van doesn't move. Kevin looks out of the front window to see nothing but a starlit sky.

Crystal opens the side door and calls out to Kevin.

"Hand her over to me, slowly," Crystal says.

Kevin looks down. His penis is going through the bullet hole in the top of Stephanie's mouth as she blows him. He imagines that if she didn't have so much hair he would be able to see the tip of it coming out of the exit wound.

This is fucked, he thinks.

He looks at Crystal, "I can't."

"This thing is going to go over the side at any minute," she says.

Kevin feels like he is about to have an orgasm. This makes him pause for a moment. Part of him thinks that if he is going to die anyway then dying during a blowjob is the way to go. The more sensible side of him thinks that he has to do everything in his power to save Stephanie. He wonders what the doctors (or coroners) will think if they find his semen inside of her skull once they get to the hospital.

He wonders what the heck happened to Stephanie. He wonders why she is acting like this. She seems completely unaware of what is going on around her. It is like the bullet has scrambled her brain.

As he pulls himself out of her mouth and pushes her away, Stephanie lunges forward with all her strength, kicking off of the side door to get closer to him. The van shakes and slides farther over the edge. Crystal shrieks at them.

"What the hell are you doing?" Crystal cries. "Get out!"

Kevin wriggles out of Stephanie's grip and opens his door. Without thinking, he jumps out of the van and lands on the rocky side of the cliff. Only half of his body makes it. His legs dangle over the edge.

Crystal can't get to Kevin to help him up. They are separated by the van, the side of the mountain, and the drop-off. He has to pull himself up, scraping his naked penis across a jagged rock as he gets to safety. When he rolls over and looks at his dick, it is covered in blood. He isn't sure if he just cut it open or if it is blood from Stephanie's head wound. He decides to zip up his pants and worry about it later.

Stephanie doesn't know where Kevin went. She sits up and looks around. She sees Crystal outside the van calling out to her through the side door. She can't understand what she is saying.

"Come on, Steph," Crystal says like she is talking to a puppy. "Come on."

Stephanie crawls over the seat. The van slips and shakes. Crystal tries to hold the van from sliding any further. The closer Stephanie gets to Crystal, the quicker the van starts to move.

Jason is on the ground crying silently in agony. When he hit the ground, his kneecap popped out of joint. His underwear soaks up the wet mud as he tries to figure out a way to undo the dislocation of his knee. He looks around. The sound of croaking frogs is loud around him. It is like they are screaming. Screaming at him to get off of his feet and get out of there. Nobody is going to find him. He's all alone. The only person who is going to help him is himself. The wind shakes the trees and freezes the moisture on his body.

He straightens his leg out and hears a popping noise from inside of his leg as his kneecap slides back into place. Standing himself up, he puts all of his weight on his good leg. Then he unzips his fanny pack and pulls out the pistol.

As he walks, he realizes that his leg isn't as badly damaged as he thought it would be. He's afraid he'll dislocate it again if he puts too much weight on it, but he is able to move around without too much of a limp. He steps through the trees, looking up the side of the cliff at the cabin's lights so that he can find his way to the bodies.

When Kevin gets off of the ground and looks through the van's windows, he sees Crystal on the other side, pulling Stephanie off of the back seat to safety. The van stops sliding. It settles into place. He doesn't know how he's going to get to them with the van blocking the path. He could try to climb up the steep slope behind him, but decides it might be best to hold off just in case the van does go over the cliff.

"Is she okay?" Kevin calls out.

Crystal is busy holding Stephanie back. For some reason, the wounded girl is trying to get back into the van. Her eyes are wild and bloody drool leaks down her chin. Once Steph settles down, Crystal says, "She's messed up."

"Take her back to the cabin," Kevin says. "I'll go down the mountain and call for help."

"We're coming with you," Crystal says.

"You're not going to drag her all the way down the mountain in the dark," he says. "Either take her back to the cabin or wait here. I'll go as fast as I can."

Kevin turns and jogs away from them.

"Wait," Crystal calls out, holding back Stephanie from getting into the van. It seems to her that Stephanie is trying to crawl through the van so that she can go with Kevin. "I need your help."

Kevin doesn't stop.

"I'll get help as soon as I can," he says.

Crystal calls out again, but he's already gone.

When Jason gets to the section of cliff directly under the cabin, he searches the area for the creature's body. He doesn't find anything. He moves slowly and quietly, pointing his gun at every branch that blows in the breeze and every frog that croaks. He combs the area foot by foot, but there's nothing. No blood. No bodies.

He doesn't know what he's going to do if the gray man is still alive. He has put several bullets in his chest, one in his brain, one in the fetus' brain. If that mixed with a twenty story drop isn't enough to kill the creature then he doesn't know what is.

After nearly half an hour of searching, Jason does find a body. He finds Rick's corpse up in the trees. It never hit the ground. Rick was impaled by a thick pine branch pointing straight up from the tree's trunk like an index finger with a long pointed fingernail. The branch went into Rick's new vagina, cut through his body, and came out of his mouth. His body slid several feet down the pole of wood, turning him into a human kebob. Jason cringes at the sight of his friend's corpse, but he does not look away. He pretends not to be bothered by it, even though it is the most disturbing thing he's ever seen. It looks incredibly painful. He tries not to imagine how painful his death must have been, hoping that Rick died instantly and didn't suffer for very long like that. He wonders if his dad would approve of him hoping that his friend didn't suffer.

There's no sign of Desdemona's body, but he does see a pile of bloody pine needles ten feet away from him. Jason limps over to the pile and examines the blood. He touches it to make sure it is real. There is a trail of blood leading away from this spot. It goes towards the river.

Jason takes a deep breath. He doesn't know how, but the thing must still be alive. That is, unless there is another one of them out in these woods who dragged the gray man's body away. He decides to follow the blood.

One way or another, he thinks, *I'm going to kill that thing for good.*

Desdemona is in midair, hanging from the balcony of the cabin, holding on for her life. She didn't fall all the way to the ground with the others. As she fell, a strand of her intestine hooked onto the wooden rail and saved her from the drop. She is surprised that her intestine is able to hold her weight. She is surprised that she is still alive at all.

Her hands slip down her intestine as she tries to climb it, holding on with as tight of a grip as possible so that she doesn't slide so far that more of her innards will be pulled out of her abdomen. She tries to focus on climbing. She tries not to think about Rick. She watched in agony as her boyfriend and the gray man slipped out of her grasp and fell to their deaths. She heard Rick cry out to her as he fell, but there was nothing she could do. She was lucky to have survived herself.

She also tries to block Jason out of her mind. Every time she thinks of Jason she gets so angry that it distracts her from climbing. She wants to kill Jason for shooting Rick.

She doesn't care if it was an accident. She also wants to kill him for not seeing her dangling from the balcony. Des watched as Jason stepped to the balcony's edge and peered down, looking straight at her, but for some reason didn't notice she was there. She tried to call to him for help, but she wasn't able to speak. It felt as if her throat had been ripped out.

The balcony is only about nine feet above her, but it is difficult for her to pull herself up such a slippery rope. She climbs up a couple feet and then slides down three. Blood flows out of her neck and mouth, wetting her chest. The wind freezes her skin into gooseflesh. Her whines ooze out of her mouth with the blood. As she cries, she can feel her voice box vibrating on the outside of her neck.

With all her strength she forces herself to climb five feet up the intestine, but then she slides down four feet before she can reach even the bottom of the balcony.

Crystal sits with Stephanie for nearly an hour by the side of the van. The engine is still running and the lights are still on. She doesn't plan to try to turn it off. Stephanie babbles in a drunken language that doesn't sound remotely English. The only thing Crystal understands is "I eat Pete" which she believes is supposed to be "I need to sleep."

"I eat Pete," Stephanie says, rolling her eyes. "I jut eat Pete. Sane all."

"You can't sleep," Crystal says. "You've got to stay

awake. You could die if you fall asleep."

"Jut Pete," Stephanie says.

"Kevin will get you help soon," Crystal says. "Just hang on."

Stephanie lays her head on Crystal's shoulder, squishing brain goop onto her neck. When Crystal realizes the bloody mess is touching her she jumps away, shrieking like a spider had just crawled down her shirt. Stephanie looks at her drunkenly, confused about what is going on, as Crystal tries to rub the blood off of her neck with the bottom of her shirt.

Her whines go silent as she hears something in the distance. At first she thinks it's a rescue vehicle bouncing against rocky terrain as it comes up the mountain towards her. But as she listens carefully, she realizes it's not that. It is the sound of gun shots. She hears Jason's voice in the distance. She listens carefully. The sound isn't coming from the cabin. It is coming from below her, at the bottom of the cliff. There are more gunshots. The voice becomes louder. She can make out some of the words. Whoever it is, he is swearing at the top of his lungs and shooting at something. She's not sure, but she thinks it sounds exactly like Jason.

"But it can't be him," she says.

Crystal goes to Stephanie and picks her up off of the ground. She doesn't like touching the girl with all of the blood on her body but is willing to put up with it to save her life.

"Come on," Crystal says. "We're going back to the cabin."

Jason is hunting something in the dark. It is moving fast for something that has just been hit with so many bullets. It is leaving a bloody trail for him to follow. He isn't sure if this creature is the same one that fell off the cliff or if it is something new. He could be chasing after a deer for all he knows.

The thing won't die, whatever it is. Jason limps after it as fast as he can, putting as many bullets into the creature as possible, pretending that his ammunition is an unlimited supply.

"I eat Pete!" Stephanie cries in her half-sleep.

Stephanie is able to walk on her own, but she stumbles and wavers a lot. Crystal has to help her balance as she moves, as she has done with so many of her drunken friends after parties before. But Stephanie is a little different from the drunks she has walked home in the past. She doesn't only stumble and sway, she also occasionally spasms like electricity is going down her spine and sometimes her eyes quiver back and forth as if she is going through rapid eye movement with her eyes open.

"Stop saying that," Crystal says.

Crystal hurries them up the hill. She's not sure if Jason is drunk and messing around with the gun to kill time or if there are other people out in the woods with them, but she'll feel a lot safer if she can get back to the cabin with the others.

Above her, on top of the hillside to her right, Crystal sees what looks to be somebody standing there, looking down on her. She is sure that she is just imagining things, but the closer she gets to it the more it resembles a human figure.

As they pass underneath the thing, Crystal picks up the pace and pulls Stephanie with as much force as she can. Stephanie doesn't fight it. Once the figure is behind them, Crystal looks back. It clearly looks like a person up there. A naked person with very pale skin. Then she sees the thing move. It brings its hand up to its face, then rubs its hand across its bald head.

"Come on," Crystal whispers to Stephanie as she tries to get her to run.

Stephanie resists. She is completely unaware of the figure. She whines loudly at her in an incomprehensible babble, forcing Crystal to cover her mouth so that the thing won't hear them. Stephanie cries out and bites her friend's finger.

The naked person is attracted by Stephanie's voice. It climbs down the hill like a monkey and crabwalks into the path behind them.

What the fuck? Crystal says to herself.

She keeps moving, pushing Stephanie forward by the back of her neck. Stephanie fights her the whole way.

Crystal wonders what that thing could be. An idea comes into her head. She wonders if the thing isn't alone. She wonders if there are dozens of them in the woods, surrounding them. She wonders if Jason was chased away from the cabin into the woods by them. Perhaps what she heard was her boyfriend running for his life out there in the woods, trying to fight his way to the highway. She wonders if anyone will be in the cabin at all when she gets there.

Once the lights of the cabin come into view in the distance, she looks back. There's nothing there. She hopes that the thing was just her imagination. She's heard that this level of stress is likely to cause the strangest of hallucinations.

The closer they get to the cabin, the slower Stephanie becomes.

"Stay awake," Crystal tells her as she attempts to keep her friend upright.

"Jut go," Stephanie says, her voice becoming faint.

Stephanie's legs go limp and she drops to the ground. She sighs all of her breath out of her lungs and curls up around Crystal's feet.

Crystal shakes her. "Come on."

Stephanie closes her eyes and her consciousness drifts away.

"Come on," Crystal says, looking at the path behind them to make sure nothing is coming. "You can't go to sleep. Come on, Steph. Get up."

Stephanie doesn't react to her. Her limbs are like rubber.

Crystal can no longer hear her breathing. She puts her hand over her chest but can't feel a heartbeat. She's dead.

Crystal's eyes fill with water, but before she can cry something grabs her attention. The figure is back. It is coming down the dirt road towards her. She can get a good view of it now. It isn't exactly human. It is some kind of mutant. It is a seven-foot-tall pot-bellied naked woman with sagging wrinkled breasts, a bald head, and two tiny holes for nostrils.

The gray-skinned woman holds out her hands. Her arms are much longer than normal human arms. They are almost the same length as her legs. On each hand, she has three fingers and two thumbs. She has extra thumbs where her pinky fingers should be. There are long metal blades on each of her fingers and metal hooks on each of her thumbs.

When she sees the claws, Crystal turns and runs. She doesn't know if the creature chases after her or not. She just runs.

As she dashes for the cabin, she notices that the front door has been ripped off and is lying in the dirt. All of the outside lights have been smashed. The lighting inside is dim. A gray blur bullets past her and darts into the cabin through the broken door.

The thing was fast. It looked like the mutant creature that was behind Crystal but it moved so quickly that she isn't sure what it was. Crystal stops and looks back. Nothing is behind her. She wonders if the thing really went inside. She wonders if she is hallucinating all of this.

She steps through the doorway of the cabin and looks in. She doesn't see anything in the entryway. Just in case the thing really is real and inside the cabin, Crystal decides she needs a weapon. The only things in the entryway are those weird bronzed hands growing out of the wall. Crystal pulls on one of them. It is hard and heavy enough to make a decent weapon, but she can't get it out of the wall.

Listening carefully, there doesn't seem to be any sounds coming from around the corner. The entire cabin is silent. She decides to go forward, unarmed, stepping carefully into the living room.

The living room and kitchen are empty. Crystal sneaks into the kitchen and takes a butcher knife out of a grocery bag filled with utensils. She looks for the gun that had been on the kitchen counter. It is gone. All of the bullets are gone as well, except for one that is lying on the kitchen floor.

There is a bubbling noise coming from somewhere in the next room. Crystal peers over the kitchen counter and scans the living room area, but there is nobody in there. Then she sees movement coming from the other side of the couch and looks closely.

She sees the back of Des's mohawk.

Desdemona is sitting on the couch, drinking from Jason's bottle of scotch. Crystal comes up behind her.

"Des!"

Crystal lowers the knife and sighs with relief as she sees her friend drinking casually on the couch. She thinks she must have hallucinated that ghostly gray figure. *It wasn't outside and it didn't come in here. It wasn't real.* Crystal has had hallucinations caused by stress before. One time, when she was in charge of organizing a homecoming party, she became so stressed out that she heard voices the entire day. It was her own voice that she heard, telling her things that she needed to do to make the party perfect, but it sounded like it was coming from another person standing behind her talking over her shoulder. With all that had happened with Stephanie, Crystal believes it's very possible that these could have been stress-related hallucinations.

"Steph didn't make it, Des," Crystal says softly.

Des turns to her with the bottle in her mouth.

"I left her outside," Crystal says.

As Crystal steps around the side of the couch, she sees Desdemona's entrails spread out across the cushions and the carpeting. Her friend is covered in blood. Her throat has been ripped open and a stream of Johnny Walker Red is dribbling out.

"What the fuck happened?" Crystal cries. "Des! Holy shit!"

Desdemona blinks slowly and brings the bottle of scotch down to her lap, getting it tangled in her pile of mud-caked intestines.

"Where is everyone?" Crystal cries. "What in the hell is going on?"

"Something in the woods," Desdemona croaks through her broken larynx.

"Where's Rick and Jason?"

"Rick is dead," Desdemona wheezes. "Jason took off."

Crystal goes to her friend and tries to comfort her, but she doesn't want to touch her mess.

"Don't worry, Des," Crystal says. "Kevin is going for help. I'm sure he's already called the cops by now. It shouldn't be long before they send in a rescue helicopter. You'll be fine."

"I won't be fine," Desdemona says.

Crystal jerks her head back and looks around the room, as she remembers the gray mutant who she'd seen enter the cabin moments before. She retrieves her butcher knife and goes to Desdemona, lowering her voice to a whisper.

"Did you see anything come through here before me?" Crystal says.

Desdemona shakes her head.

"It was this naked mutant woman with long arms and metal fingernails," she says. "Is that the thing that did this to you?"

Desdemona shakes her head. "It wasn't a woman."

"There's more of them?" Crystal asks.

"I thought there was only one," Desdemona says.

Crystal leaves Desdemona in the living room to search the house for the gray-skinned woman. The upstairs is dark and quiet. She decides to make sure the ground floor is safe before heading up there.

She wonders how many of the creatures there are. There are at least two, but the cabin could be surrounded by those things. She doesn't like leaving Desdemona alone in the living room, especially with the front door of the cabin ripped off, but she doesn't want to force her friend to move. Stephanie might not have died if she wasn't dragged back and forth through the woods. Crystal didn't want to make that mistake again.

There is a noise coming from down the hallway. It is the sound of tools falling from shelves. The room where Stephanie was supposed to sleep is empty, but across the hall, under the stairs, there is an open door that shouldn't be open. It is the door that leads down into the basement.

Crystal steps slowly down the stairs into the basement, carrying the butcher knife at her waist like a sheathed sword. The generator is purring loud enough to hide the creaking of the wooden steps as she descends.

The creature is on the other side of the room, digging through Jason's grandfather's collection of mounted deer heads and stuffed birds. The gray woman picks up a duck and bites into its breast. Sawdust spills over the creature's lips. It turns around, facing Crystal, as it tries to eat the mounted duck. Crystal gets a good look at the swollen belly of the creature. It looks as if the thing is almost nine-months pregnant and ready to burst.

Crystal slowly steps back as the creature spits feathers and woodchips into the air. It is looking straight at her. Before the creature has a chance to charge her, Crystal turns around and runs up the steps.

Once she gets upstairs, she closes the basement door and slides the latch into place to lock it. Before the latch is secure, the thing slams into the door. Crystal pushes her weight against it. The creature slams again.

"Des," she cries. "I need your help."

With the next impact, the door cracks a little in the center.

"Des!"

Her friend doesn't answer.

Crystal decides to make a run for it. She leaps away from the door and rushes into the living room. Desdemona is no longer on the couch. The room is empty.

"Des!" she yells, but she doesn't wait around for a response.

She runs up the stairs to the third floor and heads straight for the attic. The sound of the creature slamming on the door echoes up the stairway. She pulls the cord on the ceiling and climbs up the ladder.

Dashing blindly into the dark of the attic, her feet catch on one of the pinball-boy sculptures, the one that Kevin drew the smiley face on. She trips and slams her head into one of the bowling balls hanging from the ceiling.

While she sits there in the dark, her hands coated in dust, blood gushing out of her nose, she debates whether or not she should just close the attic door and hide up there until morning. If the cabin is surrounded with these creatures, she doesn't stand a chance. Rick and Stephanie are dead. Jason and Desdemona are missing, presumed dead. Kevin is either long gone or never made it down the hill. She's all alone. She is better off just hiding.

But she doesn't like the idea of sitting in a dark attic all night. She just can't get herself to do it. Right now, she has a creature locked in the basement. If she can reinforce the door the thing will be trapped down there. For all she knows, this is the only one she has to worry about. For all she knows, it is the only one still alive. She's got to keep it locked in the basement.

CHAPTER SIX
KEVIN

Kevin puts his hand in his pants, trying to rub the crusted blood off the head of his penis as he hikes up the hill back to the cabin. He had called 911 and they said that forest rangers would be there shortly. He asked if they could send in a rescue chopper, but they said that the forest rangers will be able to get there sooner. By the tone of her voice, the operator didn't sound very optimistic about Stephanie's chances. She acted as though she'd never even heard of anyone surviving a gunshot wound to the head.

"Are you sure she shot herself in the head?" said the operator in an annoyed voice. She thought Kevin was playing a practical joke.

"Yes."

"The bullet went into her head?"

"Half her fucking head is gone."

"Don't you swear to me."

"Half her head is gone."

"And she's alive?"

"Yes."

"Are you sure?"

"Yes."

"Okay . . . If you say so, kid."

It was such a ridiculous experience. He wonders if he should sue them if Stephanie dies because of their negligence. He wonders if Stephanie has a chance even if they weren't negligent.

Kevin has HIV. He hasn't told anyone yet. He's not sure if he's ever going to. Des and Rick had no idea that Kevin cheated on them during most of junior year. He cheated on them all the time. Kevin really liked having sex with Des and Rick, at first, because they were the ones who introduced him to sex. But he actually wasn't very attracted to them. He was only with them because he didn't want to lose them as friends. Once he started sleeping around, he realized that he liked having sex with other people a lot more.

He got HIV from some hood rat that he fucked when he was really drunk at a party one time. He was too drunk to care to wear a condom and the girl was too drunk to realize that he didn't use a condom. After they finished, and the girl noticed he wasn't wearing protection, she flipped out.

She said, "Why the fuck didn't you wear a condom?"

He said, "I don't know."

She said, "I have HIV."

He said, "What?"

She said, "You fucked up."

He said, "Why the fuck would you have sex with me if you knew you had HIV?"

She said, "I thought you'd wear a condom. Everybody knows I have HIV."

Later, he got tested, just to be sure, and the result was positive.

He didn't tell Des or Rick that he had contracted the virus, but he continued to sleep with them. Without protection. He didn't want them to know he had HIV or that he had been cheating on them, because he was worried that they might not want to be friends with him anymore. So he gave them HIV. He figured that it would be best if the three of them had it together.

Once the others find out, he will pretend he has no idea how they got it. He thinks that since they are in a threesome relationship, nobody will exactly know who brought the STD into the group. Desdemona won't know if it was Rick or Kevin. Rick won't know if it was Desdemona or Kevin. Kevin will pretend he thinks it's either Rick or Desdemona. In the end, they will be forced to forgive and forget. Then they will move on and focus on living with HIV together.

As Kevin walks up the dirt road in the dark, he wonders if he had just given Stephanie HIV when she had his penis in her brain. He doesn't like the idea of Stephanie having to live with both severe brain damage and HIV. He wonders if it would be better for her if she didn't survive the night.

Crystal collects a handful of nails and puts them into

her pocket. Then she grabs a hammer with her butcher knife hand and off the wall takes a couple of boards that were being used as shelves. She can still hear the banging of the basement door as she goes down the stairway. She has no idea why the door hasn't broken yet. That creature looked very strong and the latch on the door looked pretty weak.

Once she gets downstairs, she finds Desdemona leaning against the basement door with the Theremin to keep the creature inside.

"Where the hell were you?" Desdemona croaks.

"Where the hell were you?" Crystal responds.

They nail the boards across the door. Then they break apart the Theremin cabinet and use the wood to secure the door even further. The creature shrieks on the other side. It continues to slam and claw at the door.

"Let's put the couch in front of it," Desdemona says.

Crystal agrees.

Desdemona drapes her entrails over the couch as they carry it to the basement door. The couch is wide enough that it takes up most of the width of the hall. They only need to stuff a few chairs in front of it to keep it locked in place.

"Is that good enough?" Crystal says.

"There's no way it can get the door open," Des croaks. "It'll have to break the door into pieces in order to get out."

"We should keep reinforcing it," Crystal says.

Desdemona agrees.

Crystal runs outside to grab the front door out of the dirt. She thinks nailing the door across the basement door will be enough to do the trick. Before she gets the door inside, a figure staggers out of the woods towards her. She drops the door and holds up her butcher knife and the hammer.

"Crystal . . ." says the figure.

She recognizes Jason's voice. He steps into the light. His half-naked body is covered in dirt and large bloody gashes.

"What happened?" Crystal says, rushing into the woods to great him.

She helps him limp into the cabin. His knee has swollen to the size of a baseball from moving around on it so much after the dislocation, so he can hardly walk on it anymore.

Jason is completely exhausted. Between heavy breaths he says, "The thing won't die. No matter how many bullets I put in him, he won't stay dead."

"Where is it?" Crystal says. "Are there more of them?"

"Behind me," he says. "It's following me."

Crystal looks into the woods, but doesn't see anything.

"It's been keeping its distance but I think it followed me all the way back here," he says. "I don't think it realized I was out of bullets. If it had I would've been dead for sure."

"We have one in the basement," Crystal says. "A different one. A female."

"There's more of those things?" Jason asks.

"Des and I are barricading the door so that it can't get out."

"Desdemona's alive?" he says. "How the fuck is Desdemona still alive?"

"Stephanie didn't make it," Crystal says. "Kevin went down the mountain to get help."

Jason helps Crystal nail the loose door over the basement door. The creature bangs and scratches on the other side. Desdemona stands in the hallway with her guts in her arms, glaring at Jason.

"You motherfucker," Desdemona says.

Jason doesn't look at her as he hammers a nail.

"You should have fucking died out there, you fucking bitch," Desdemona says.

Jason turns to meet her glare.

"What the hell's wrong with you?" he says.

"What's wrong with me? What's wrong with you?" Desdemona flicks intestinal juice at him.

"What's your problem?"

"Don't act like you don't know, asshole."

"What are you talking about, Des?" Crystal says.

Desdemona spits blood at the wall. Then she says, "For starters, he left me hanging off of the balcony. I had to climb my own guts to get back up."

Jason wipes the blood from his face.

"Is that true?" Crystal asks.

"And he shot Rick," Desdemona says.

"What?" Crystal cries.

Jason keeps hammering as he speaks. "You're fucking crazy. I never shot Rick. And I'm sorry if I left you hanging from the balcony. I didn't see you."

"Sure you didn't fucking see me," Desdemona says. "Just as you didn't see your bullet going into Rick's chest."

Jason finishes hammering the door and turns to her. "What do you want from me? An apology or something? Rick would have died whether I shot him or not. You were going to survive whether I helped you or not. What's the big fucking deal here? You should be happy you're even alive after all the shit that's happened to you."

Desdemona says, "I wish I could lock you in the basement with that thing. We'd see how tough you really are."

Jason turns to her and points his hammer at her face. "Bring it on, bitch. I ain't afraid of shit."

Crystal gets between them.

"You two need to cool it," Crystal says. "You can argue over this once we're safe."

"Once we're safe I'll have him arrested," Desdemona says.

Jason hits the wall with the hammer. "You even think about it and I'll make sure you don't get out of here alive."

Before Crystal can say something to keep the peace between them, Jason throws the hammer across the room and staggers upstairs.

"Fucking cunt," he mumbles to himself.

Desdemona and Crystal sit on the floor in the living room, passing the bottle of scotch between them. This is the first time Crystal hasn't been bothered by sharing a bottle with another person. The thing in the basement has stopped screaming and attacking the basement door. The creature's silence makes Desdemona nervous.

"Do you think it found another way out?" Desdemona says.

"There's no windows down there," Crystal says. "There's only one way out."

"Why did it stop?" Desdemona asks.

Crystal looks at the ground when she responds. She doesn't like to watch Des when she talks, because she can see her vocal chords vibrating through the opening in her throat.

"It probably ran out of energy. I'm pretty sure the thing is pregnant. It probably doesn't have the stamina to keep that up for very long."

"What happens when she gets her energy back? That door isn't going to last forever."

"Hopefully Kevin will be back with the cops before it breaks."

"I hope there aren't any axes or sledgehammers down there to speed up the process," Desdemona says.

"I doubt that monster knows how to use such things," Crystal says.

Desdemona nods and dribbles scotch out of her neck.

Jason is up in the attic, digging through boxes. He is frustrated that he can't find his grandfather's guns. He knows that the old man had tons of guns in this place, but they are all missing. If he just had some more bullets he wouldn't need another gun, but there aren't any left in the gun cabinet.

After dust and cobwebs get mixed with the blood on his body, he punches a hole in the wall. He doesn't know what else to do. He's irritated and angry. He kicks a pinball boy statue across the room with his good leg. While putting all of his weight on his bad leg, an incredible pain shoots up his thigh. The pain gets him even more pissed. He takes one of the bowling balls hanging from the ceiling and swings it around like a ball and chain. He uses it to slam more holes in the walls and smash a pinball sculpture.

He staggers downstairs and takes the bottle of scotch away from the girls.

"I can't find the guns anywhere," he says, then takes a swig from the bottle.

"Maybe you should look in the basement," Desdemona says, giggling apathetically.

Jason flips her off while he continues to drink.

The creature in the basement howls.

139

"What the hell is it doing that for?" Jason says.

The howls are piercing. Crystal puts her fingers in her ears.

"It sounds like a wolf," Desdemona says.

Jason stares at the door, waiting for the thing to burst out.

"Maybe it's calling for help," Crystal says. "Holy shit . . .What if more of them will come?"

"Shoot the damn thing through the door," Desdemona says.

The creature's howls become louder. They have to yell at the tops of their lungs in order to hear each other.

"I'm out of bullets," Jason says.

"There's one on the kitchen floor," Crystal says.

She rushes into the kitchen and fetches the bullet for Jason.

"It's the last one," she says as she hands it to him. "Better make it count."

Jason nods. He loads the pistol and then goes to the basement door. He points at where he thinks the howling is coming from.

"Hurry up," Desdemona says. "Before it attracts more of those things here."

Jason hesitates. His gun trembles.

"Shoot!" Desdemona says.

"What's wrong?" Crystal says.

Jason shakes his head and lowers the pistol.

"I can't," he says.

"Why not?" Crystal says.

"It's my last bullet," he says. "I can't waste it."

"Can't *waste* it?" Crystal cries.

He says, "That thing is trapped down there. It's not a threat to us. We need to save the bullet for the other one."

"For all we know, there could be hundreds of those things outside," Desdemona says, coiling her guts around her tattooed fingers nervously. "If you can kill this one now it might stop them all from coming here."

Jason shakes his head. "I'm not wasting it."

"That one bullet is going to be worthless against dozens of those things," Crystal says.

Jason steps away from the basement door. "We only know about two of them. I don't think there are any more than that. This one is probably just calling for her mate."

Crystal looks at Desdemona, then back at Jason. "Well, it is . . . pregnant."

"See," Jason says. "I'm right. It's just calling for its mate."

The thing's howls grow so loud they rattle the walls.

Jason has to speak close to Crystal's ears. "We're going to take advantage of having that thing trapped in the basement. It's going to bring the male freak straight to us. We just have to wait. Once it gets here we'll ambush it."

Crystal gives Jason a worried look. She's not interested in ambushing anything.

"It'll be fine," Jason says.

Desdemona can't hear what they are saying. She sits in a yoga position on the floor, squishing her entrails like a messy stress-ball.

The howling stops as they hear a bang against the side of the cabin. They all turn their heads towards the open doorway. It is pitch black out there. The moon has disappeared again.

"It's here," Jason says.

He raises his pistol and steps carefully towards the entryway. The girls follow close behind him. Crystal points her butcher knife forward, hiding it behind Jason's back.

"Be careful," Crystal whispers into Jason's ear.

Jason gives her an angry look and mouths the words, "Shut the fuck up."

As they get to the doorway and peek their heads outside, a white blur jumps in front of them and yells "Booyah!"

Jason fires the gun a split second before he realizes that it is Kevin. The bullet hits him in the chest and Kevin hits the ground.

"Kevin!" Desdemona screams. She runs to him. She spills her intestines onto his belly as she lifts his head off of the ground and hugs him into her messy breast.

Turning her head to Jason, Desdemona screams, "You fucking idiot. You shot him. You shot Rick and now you shot Kevin."

"I didn't know it was him," Jason cries.

Kevin coughs up blood, staring at the hole in his chest, saying, "What the fuck . . ."

"Why the hell did he jump out like that?" Jason cries. "What the hell is his problem?"

"He doesn't know about the creatures yet," Crystal says.

Crystal kneels down and blows on the side of Kevin's face to get his attention. He's in shock. He turns one eye towards her.

"Kevin," Crystal says, "I need you to answer very carefully. If you can't speak, just nod."

Kevin slowly nods.

"Did you call the police?" Crystal says.

Kevin nods.

"Will they be here soon?" Crystal says.

Kevin nods.

"Are they sending a helicopter?" Crystal says.

Kevin shakes his head.

"Are they sending cops?"

Kevin shakes his head.

"They're just sending an ambulance?"

Kevin shakes his head.

"Then what the hell is coming?"

Kevin opens his mouth to release a mouthful of bloody drool. "Forest ranger."

"That's it?" Crystal says. "A fucking forest ranger?"

Kevin's eyes flutter and begin to go limp.

Desdemona slaps his face lightly. "Stay with me."

Kevin says, "How's Stephanie?"

"You didn't see her body on the way here?" Crystal says.

Kevin closes his eyes and shakes his head.

"Let's get him inside," Desdemona says.

Crystal helps Des lift Kevin's body. Kevin drifts in and out of consciousness.

"I can't believe they are only sending a fucking forest ranger," Crystal says.

"It's probably a law enforcement ranger," Jason says. He doesn't help them, but leads the way as they bring Kevin into the cabin. "Those guys are like cops, firefighters, and paramedics all rolled into one. If they send a bunch of those guys out here we'll be good to go. If they only send one, at least we'll—"

Jason is cut off by a shrieking figure that jumps out of the darkness behind them. It is the gray man. He comes at them faster and fiercer than he had before. Riddled with bullet holes, dead fetus limbs hanging floppy on the sides of his head, he charges with metal lobster claws clacking.

The creature slams into Crystal, breaks Desdemona's grip on her boyfriend, and shoves them forward into the entryway of the cabin. It doesn't stop shoving until it drives Kevin's body hard against the wall.

Crystal falls on her butt. She looks up and her face gets showered with blood.

"Kevin!" Desdemona cries.

Kevin's body is limp and hanging from the wall. One of the bronze hands has impaled him. It sticks out of his chest, through his heart, hanging there like a coat on a rack in the entryway.

Des runs at the creature. She drops her guts and lets them slide out as she runs at the thing, ready to tear its eyeballs out with her bare fingers. But the thing elbows her square in the forehead, swatting her away like a fly. She soars backwards, rolls across the ground, and gets tangled in her own intestines. In half-consciousness, she can't figure out how to free herself from her flesh bondage.

The creature turns on Crystal. It picks her up off of the ground by the throat. She can feel her larynx crushing in on itself. The metal claw opens large gashes on the bottom of her cheeks, cutting all the way up the jawbone. She stares into the thing's eyes. Its eyes are wild and filled with rage. She realizes now that capturing the creature's mate was the worst possible thing they could have done.

Crystal looks over the its shoulder at her boyfriend. Jason's mouth is agape. He doesn't know what to do.

"Help me . . ." Crystal is barely able to gurgle the words out of her tightened throat.

With those words, Jason turns around and runs. He staggers upstairs as quick as he can on one leg and doesn't look back.

Crystal stabs the thing in the stomach with her butcher knife and it drops her. She crawls past its knees into the living room. It staggers after her and picks her up off of the ground again, this time by her armpit. The metal claw cuts deep into the side of her arm.

She stabs it in the stomach again, but it doesn't let her go. She stabs it in the chest. This doesn't even phase the creature.

Crystal screams for Jason, but there is no sign of Jason anywhere.

The creature in the basement howls again. At the sound of the howling noise, the gray man cries out with anger. With his free lobster claw, he cuts into one of Crystal's breasts. He squeezes and growls, cutting through the mound of meat like his claw is a pair of scissors.

Crystal shrieks and stabs the thing repeatedly in the chest. She stabs it in the face. She stabs it in the neck. But the thing won't stop cutting. Her white shirt becomes dark red. Once the claw cuts all the way through, she expects to feel a ball of flesh roll out of her shirt and plop onto the carpet. But it doesn't fall. The breast wasn't completely severed. It is still dangling by a flap of skin.

The creature takes the bloody claw from her chest and brings it up to her throat. Crystal screams as the claws squeeze together around her neck. It gurgles at Crystal as it constricts its claws to cut her head off.

Crystal closes her eyes so that she doesn't have to see her own body after she is decapitated. She knows that your brain survives for a little while after your head is cut off. She knows you can look up and see your headless body standing above you. This is not something she wants to experience. It is just too gross.

After she went through puberty, Crystal started thinking everything was gross. She didn't like the smells and textures of things. She didn't like to look at things that were ugly. But when she was a kid, she was quite the opposite.

She didn't think anything was gross.

As a kid, Crystal loved to play with bugs and reptiles. She liked to collect them and hide them in her room in little jars under her bed. There were dozens of them. Snakes, frogs, lizards, spiders, beetles, cockroaches, June bugs. Sometimes, at night when everyone else was asleep, she would let her little creatures out of their jars. She would bring them all under the covers with her and let them crawl all over her body. She liked how it felt to be tickled and touched by all of the little things.

As she grew a little older, Crystal started swallowing the animals alive so that she could feel them tickle the inside of her body. She started with little spiders, then tadpoles, and then salamanders. She liked the idea of something living and then dying inside of her. She especially liked the idea of things dying.

After that, Crystal's favorite activity was to kill things that were smaller than her. Following a rainstorm, her family's porch used to be crawling with dozens and dozens of snails. She loved the sound it made when she would step on the snails and crush them. After that, she would collect baby frogs by the pond in her backyard. She would come up with imaginative new ways to kill each of the frogs. Sometimes she would even invent a story to go along with each death or create names and character traits for each of them. When it came to the part of the story where one of the amphibians had to die, she would step on it, smash it with a rock, throw it against the side of her house, bite its head off, swallow it alive, sit on it, burn it on a stake, stab it with a pencil, cover it in melted candle wax, drop it down the garbage disposal, or cut it in half with her paper-cutter.

She didn't realize what a gruesome game it was that

she was playing, but she enjoyed it. Eventually, Crystal moved on to bigger things. She liked to throw rocks at birds and snakes until they died. She liked to catch the neighborhood cats and suffocate them in a green garbage bag or strangle them with an old television cord.

She never regretted killing any of the animals. It was just a thing she did for fun. She didn't even regret the time she took her neighbor's pet golden retriever out of their backyard. The dog was excited to see her, wagging its tail, carrying a chewed up red Frisbee in its mouth. She stabbed it in the neck four times with a rusty screwdriver and then sawed its head off while it was still partially alive. The neighbors found their dog's headless body later that day. Crystal could hear them screaming and crying through the fence, but she didn't understand why.

As the gray man cuts into her neck, Crystal thinks about the dog that she killed that day. She wonders if this is what it felt like.

Before the metal claw hits a major artery, Jason comes down the stairs. He has one of the bowling balls attached to a chain that had been hanging in the attic. He swings it over his head, and then releases it at the creature's legs.

The gray creature's knee makes a loud cracking sound and it goes down. The thing screams in agony. Jason lifts the bowling ball and slams it into the thing's leg again with all of his strength. The leg breaks. Jason can see the bones separate under the flesh.

Crystal holds her neck and tumbles backwards, crawling away from the thing on the ground. The creature in the basement scratches furiously on the basement door, trying to get out to save her mate.

"You think you're tough, bitch?" Jason says to the creature. "I'll show you tough."

He swings the ball and chain at the thing's head. It hits with a loud thump and the freak stops screaming. Its eyes sag and it becomes dizzy. Jason grabs one of the creature's fetus legs and rips it off of the side of his head like an earring. The creature cries out again. Jason slams the bowling ball into its mouth, shattering its three front teeth.

"You think you can fucking kill me?" Jason yells, as he strikes the creature again with the bowling ball. "You can't kill me, bitch. I will fucking kill you."

Jason smashes the ball and chain into the creature repeatedly, breaking his bones into splinters, pounding his face into pulp.

The thing on the ground whimpers at Jason's feet but it just won't die.

"Why won't you die, bitch?" Jason says.

He stops bludgeoning the creature and pulls its head into his face.

Only an inch away from the creature's ear, Jason says, "I'll show you that there are things far worse than death."

Jason bends the broken creature over, pulls down his whitey-tighties, and shoves his penis deep into the thing's asshole. The creature shrieks and struggles, but it is too damaged to push Jason out.

"That's right, bitch," Jason says. "You fuck with me and I'll fucking rape you."

Crystal watches in shock and awe as her boyfriend fucks the creature. The sight both disturbs and excites her. Jason ass-rapes the thing just as violently as he was beating it with the bowling ball. He punches it in the kidneys as it whines and whimpers for mercy. He rips on its dead fetus arms to make it scream louder.

The female creature in the basement wails and howls, thrashing at the door, but she can do nothing to stop Jason from molesting her mate.

Jason's father wasn't afraid of anything. Not a single thing. It was his goal in life to make sure that Jason was not afraid of anything, either. Whenever he learned of something Jason was afraid of, he would make him face that fear. When Jason was a kid, he was afraid of the dark, so his dad locked him in a closet for a weekend. When Jason showed a fear of spiders, his dad put his hand in a black widow's web so that it would crawl onto his hand and bite him. When Jason showed that he had a fear of being picked on or beaten up, his dad paid three kids that were two grades older to bully him every day until he wasn't afraid of them anymore and finally fought back.

The one that bothered Jason the most was when he was in junior high, the time that his dad discovered that he was homophobic.

His dad said, "What the fuck is so scary about a faggot?"

Jason replied, "I'm not scared of them. I just think

homos are gross. There's a huge difference."

"What's so gross about them?"

"Butt sex is disgusting."

"Do you think fucking a woman in the ass is disgusting?"

"No."

"Then why would two faggots fucking disgust you? It is exactly the same thing. It's just a dick fucking an asshole. You're not disgusted, you're afraid."

"I'm not afraid!" Jason said.

"You're afraid to be around faggots. You're afraid people might suspect you are a faggot if you are okay with faggots. You're afraid that you might actually be a faggot and don't know it yet."

"No way," Jason said.

The next day, Jason's dad rented some gay porno films and forced his son to watch them. He was only thirteen years old and hadn't even seen straight porn before.

"What bothers you so much about this?" his dad said, pointing at the television screen. "It's just two men sexually gratifying each other. Just as you will do with women some day. Just as you do when you jerk off."

"Fine," Jason said. "I get it. I don't have a problem with gays anymore. Just turn it off."

"Why do you want me to turn it off?"

"Because I can't take it anymore."

"You can't take it because you're scared of it. If you were straight and you weren't scared you'd just be bored right now. If you were gay and you weren't scared you'd be turned on. Since you can't take it that means you're still scared."

"No, I'm bored," Jason said.

"Bullshit," his dad said. "I can tell when you're lying."

Jason's dad made him watch the gay porn all night long. The next day, his dad brought home a young brown-skinned male prostitute that could hardly speak English.

"I'll show you that there's nothing to be afraid of," Jason's dad said as he took off his clothes.

His dad fucked the male prostitute in the ass, right next to him on the couch in the living room, forcing him to watch.

"So what's so scary about this?" Jason's dad said as he fucked the young man.

"Nothing," Jason said.

"What is so wrong about fucking somebody in the ass?"

"Nothing," Jason said.

The prostitute didn't seem to be much older than Jason. He also didn't seem to have been a prostitute for very long. Jason watched his face as he cringed in pain. The boy closed his brown eyes as tight as he could and buried his black hair deep into the couch next to Jason.

"Are you still afraid of homosexuality?" his dad asked.

"No," Jason said.

"Then why don't you take a turn and prove it," his dad said.

Crystal's flap of breast meat smacks against the side of her chest as she gets up from the floor. She looks down into her shirt to see the mangled piece of flesh which was once her breast. It was the larger breast of the two. The one with the perfectly shaped nipple. Her favorite part of herself. She is glad that she is alive, but she feels ruined. She feels that she will never be able to go back to the Crystal she was only one night before. She wants revenge.

"Hold it down for me," Crystal says, ripping her boyfriend out of the creature.

Jason's member is covered in a foul black odor.

"Hold it down," Crystal says. "It's my turn to fuck it."

"How does it feel?" Crystal shrieks as she fucks the lobster boy with her butcher knife. "How does my dick feel in there, you freak!"

She holds the knife down to her crotch as she plunges into the creature, as if she is fucking it with a knife-shaped dick. The butcher knife stabs rapidly in and out of the creature's asshole, cutting the rectum open, leaking rivers of blood down the back of the thing's gray legs.

Jason has all of his weight on its shoulders. Crystal doesn't want to touch the creature with her skin, so he holds it down for her. While holding the mutant down, he begins to skull-fuck it. He drives his feces-coated penis into the hole on the top of the lobster boy's skull, where the fetus head used to be. He forces his member down the dead fetus throat into the creature's brain.

As they gang-rape the creature, among the moaning

and whimpering, Crystal meets Jason's gaze.

"What?" Crystal says as she knife-fucks.

"Nothing," Jason says as he skull-fucks.

She smiles. "Why are you looking at me like that?"

He smiles back. "Like what?"

"Like that."

Jason diverts his eyes and blushes. Then he looks back at Crystal.

"I was just thinking about how much I love you," Jason says.

Crystal's eyes brighten and begin to water.

"I love you, too," she says.

After Jason cums into the creature's brain, and the creature's mind becomes drunk and foggy, he says, "Want to get the other one?"

"Yeeeaah," Crystal says in a sassy voice. "That one is pregnant."

Desdemona enters the cabin with her guts thrown around her shoulders like a scarf. She diverts her eyes so that she doesn't have to see Kevin's body hanging in the entryway, then trips over the mutilated creature on the living room floor. It stares weakly at her and it gurgles, as though begging for her mercy.

Jason and Crystal enter the living room with the female creature. The thing's face is smashed and bloody, as if it had been hit with a sledgehammer a few times. Its wrists are bound with an old television cord. Crystal carries a cardboard box filled with tools from the basement.

"What's going on?" Des croaks at them.

Jason kicks the female creature's legs out from under her. "We're going to teach them a lesson."

Crystal digs through the box of tools. She pulls out a hatchet, a machete, a wood saw, a hammer, nails, a crowbar. She licks her lips and deeply inhales the metallic smell of the tools like they are roses.

"What do you need those for?" Desdemona asks.

Crystal gives a handful of nails to her boyfriend. Jason grips their prisoner tightly and holds a nail steady against one of the creature's arms, as Crystal hammers the nail through the wrist into the kitchen counter. The female screams.

"You might want to go upstairs for a while," Crystal tells Des.

The male creature gurgles and foams at them with rage. It tries to get up using its broken limbs, but can only muster up the strength to get one foot off of the floor. Jason kicks it back to the ground.

"What are you going to do?" Desdemona says.

Crystal hands the hammer to Jason and takes a swig of scotch.

"We're going to torture the bitch and force her man to watch," Crystal says, with a smile in the corner of her mouth.

After Jason nails the female's other wrist to the kitchen counter, he drags the male creature across the floor and nails its limbs to the opposite wall.

"What the fuck?" Desdemona says. "Why don't we just get out of here?"

"They deserve this," Crystal says, her eyes wild with excitement.

Des can tell there's something wrong with her best friend. She wonders if Crystal is drunk or high. She wonders if her friend has snapped.

"Just kill them and let's go," Desdemona says.

"We can't kill them," Jason says. "They won't die for some reason."

"Then tie them up or cut off their feet so they can't chase us," Desdemona says. "Let's just leave."

"We're doing this," Crystal says.

"No, you're fucking not," Desdemona says, stepping into Crystal's face.

"Go upstairs or we're going to lock you in the basement," Jason says.

"Fuck you," Desdemona says to Jason. Then she turns to Crystal. "Why would you even want to do such a thing?"

"It's going to be hot," Crystal says.

"What?" Desdemona says.

Jason stabs the machete into the female's upper thigh. Its screams make Desdemona's skin crawl.

"Stop," Desdemona says.

Jason stabs again, cutting deep. The male cries out as it watches his mate being tortured.

"This is fucking crazy," Desdemona says. "Let's go."

Crystal turns to the female and stabs at its other thigh with her butcher knife. When she stabs, she moans with sexual pleasure. Desdemona watches in horror as her friend erotically cuts open the creature's flesh.

"Stop," Desdemona says.

The two of them continue cutting and moaning,

fucking the creature with their blades.

"I said *stop*," Desdemona says.

Des leaps at her friend. She wraps her intestine around Crystal's neck and pulls her back.

"What are you doing?" Crystal cries, tugging on the rope of meat squeezed around her throat.

"What are *you* doing?" Desdemona says.

"That's it," Jason says, throwing his machete on the floor.

He staggers towards Desdemona and rips her away from Crystal. He drags her by the waist across the floor.

"Let me go, fucking asshole!" Desdemona says.

Jason tosses her into the basement and latches the door.

Desdemona almost falls down the stairs, but something holds her up as she dangles on the edge of the top step. Her intestine is caught in the door. She grabs the meaty rope and holds on for dear life. The steps are steep enough that she could break her neck if she tumbled down them backwards.

After she regains her balance, Des squats down by the basement door. She tries the handle, but it won't budge. Even though the door is no longer barricaded and the latch has been weakened, Desdemona still can't get it open. She puts her ear to the wood. There are screeching wails, flirtatious giggles, and sawing sounds coming from the living room.

They're fucking crazy, Des says to herself.

Crystal screams. Desdemona can't tell if it is a scream of agony or a scream of delight. Then there is silence.

Desdemona waits for some sound. She listens carefully. There are slight clicking noises. There are faint whimpers. The screaming, however, has stopped.

This worries Desdemona. She wonders if one of the creatures broke free. Those things could get loose and kill Jason and Crystal. If they did, Desdemona would be trapped down in the basement by herself. She decides that she needs to find a way out of there. She needs to find something in the basement to break down the basement door.

Desdemona pulls on her intestine, but can't get it free. It is completely stuck in the doorway. Shaking her head, Desdemona realizes that she has only three options. She could wait here until somebody or some*thing* opens the door for her, she could unravel the entrails out of her torso until she has enough slack to move with, or she could bite the intestine off like an animal biting off a limb to escape a hunter's trap.

She decides to go for the third option.

Desdemona didn't know the taste of her entrails would be so vile as she bites into it. She can taste salty mucous as she puts it into her mouth. The skin of the intestine makes a popping noise as it breaks open, like the skin of an Italian sausage. A glob of sour feces squeezes onto her tongue like toothpaste.

She spits it out and rubs her tongue against the wood of the door to scrape all the flavor away. The taste of shit is bad enough, but the intestine has a lining of rotten build-up that tastes of aged feety cheese mixed with road kill.

She tears through the intestine the rest of the way with her hands and then wipes the slime onto the floor.

Without the weight of her entrails, Desdemona feels lighter as she walks down the steps. She doesn't feel much pain anymore. She only feels the cold concrete under her bare feet as she reaches the bottom.

Crystal and Jason managed to take all of the tools that would have been of any use to Desdemona. She was hoping to find a pickaxe, but nothing like that is to be seen. There are many boxes, chests, and crates under the stairs. They are packed tightly and evenly, but none of them are labeled. She takes two boxes down and goes through them. They are filled with clothes. She takes several more boxes down, and goes through each of them. They are just clothes, blankets, pictures, cassette tapes. Behind the stack of boxes, Desdemona finds a red crate. She climbs onto the boxes to get it open.

Des wasn't expecting to find Jason's grandfather's gun collection. A crowbar, a hammer, or even a screwdriver would have been fine, but this arsenal is even better. They aren't packed very well, just stacked on top of each other. All of them are hunting rifles. Desdemona looks for something smaller, but can't find any handguns. She also can't find any bullets. She takes out a shotgun that was resting on the top of the pile. There aren't any shells inside. She tries another rifle, a .22 single shot. The chamber is empty. The third is a Remington semi-automatic hunting rifle. Des discovers there are some bullets in the magazine, but it isn't full. She examines the gun, tries to figure out how it works, how to unlock the safety.

The bullets don't look very big. She isn't sure if she'll be able to shoot off the latch through the basement door. She decides to use one of the heavier empty guns as a battering ram.

Desdemona breaks through the door and slips on a puddle of blood in the hallway. She gets to her feet and follows the stream of blood into the living room, where the carpet has become a red swamp and the linoleum kitchen floor is a pool of gore. Chunks of meat are scattered throughout the room.

On the wall to Desdemona's right, body parts are nailed to the wall. The parts belong to the lobster boy. He has been cut into several pieces. His arms and legs have been quartered and nailed to the wall, his torso has been skinned, stretched, and pinned up like a raccoon fur. His head is still in one piece, hanging from the wall by its dead fetus limbs. When Desdemona sees the creature, she covers her mouth with her hand.

The creature's eyes roll towards Desdemona.

Desdemona steps away. *It's still alive. Why is it still alive?*

The thing opens its mouth to speak, but it makes only a smacking sound as its tongue moves inside its lips.

There is moaning coming from the kitchen. Desdemona turns the corner to find Jason naked on the counter, licking the neck of the freak woman. The female creature is crucified to the kitchen counter. Her hands have been sawn off at the wrist. The blades of her claws have been stabbed into the sides of her ribcage, with the palms of her severed hands lying across her breasts as if they are groping her. Her legs have been cut off at the upper thigh and are curled around each other on the bloody linoleum floor like orphans cuddling together for warmth. The creature's tongue has been cut off and her lips have been stapled shut so that she couldn't scream anymore.

As he licks the freak woman's flesh, Jason caresses the woman's swollen belly with the tip of his machete. He has already cut her open from her vagina to her belly button. Crystal is lying against a wall, moaning loudly. Her eyes are locked on the pregnant monster. She is naked and masturbating with a glass dildo shaped like a baby arm. Her mouth is wide open and her tongue is licking the edges of her front teeth. Her left breast is dangling by a string of meat.

Jason digs his hands deep into the gash in the creature's belly, all the way up to his elbow, and pulls out a tiny gray arm. The fingers of the infant's hand curl softly around Jason's thumb, embracing him. Then Jason raises his machete and chops the arm off against the counter. Crystal's moans grow to a high pitch as Jason holds the severed fetus hand up for her to see.

"I'm going to cum," Crystal says. "Quick, take it out. Take it all out."

Jason nods. He puts the machete down. Then he digs into the creature's womb and rips the fetus out of her. It isn't a whole fetus. Several pieces of it have already been cut off. There are holes in its head and chest where the chunks of meat have been torn off. Jason rips the umbilical cord out of the woman's womb and lets it dangle from the mutilated fetus like a tail. The baby's cries are scratchy and a bit like television static. Besides the gray skin, the odd screams, and the pieces of flesh missing from its body, the baby isn't a mutant like its parents. It is human.

"Kill it," Crystal says, masturbating furiously now. "I want to watch you kill it."

Jason places the screaming fetus on the kitchen table, facing Crystal. The dismembered mother cries through her stapled lips, her eyes tearing and bloodshot. As Jason lifts the machete, Crystal wiggles her thighs together, pulsing against the tiny glass hand, squealing, beginning to orgasm.

Desdemona watches in horror. She isn't sure if these two people are really her friends from earlier in the day, or if they are two more creatures from the woods. All that she sees are two lunatics about to kill a baby.

"Put the knife down," Desdemona says, pointing the hunting rifle at Jason.

Jason and Crystal freeze. They look up at her. It was as if they are in some kind of rapturous trance, unaware that Desdemona had been standing there. As they snap out of it, they are shocked and angry at her interruption.

"She fucking ruined it," Crystal says, pulling her shirt back on to hide her mangled breast.

Jason steps around to the front of the table, away

from the crying infant, and faces Desdemona.

"Where did you get that?" he says.

"What the fuck's wrong with you two?" Desdemona says, her eyes watering. "You're acting like maniacs."

"I said . . ." Jason's lips are trembling with anger. "Where did you get that gun?"

"In the basement," Desdemona says.

"It's not loaded," Jason says, stepping towards her with the machete.

"Stay back," Desdemona says.

Jason keeps moving forward. Desdemona steps back.

Crystal stands up. She puts her shorts on and then goes to the female creature.

"Forget it, Jason," Crystal says, as she picks a hatchet off of the kitchen counter. "It's over. She ruined it." Then she chops the gray woman's head off in three quick strikes. It rolls off of the counter onto the kitchen floor.

"Couldn't you have waited five minutes?" Jason yells at Des.

"You're insane," Desdemona says. "You've both gone psycho."

Crystal goes to the fetus on the counter and raises the hatchet.

"I said don't move, Crystal!" Desdemona says, pointing the gun at her friend.

Crystal freezes. She rolls her eyes at Des.

"Drop the axe," Desdemona says.

Crystal drops the axe. "What the hell's your problem?"

"What the hell's your problem?" Desdemona says.

With the gun pointed at Crystal, Jason charges forward. Desdemona swings the barrel of the rifle and fires. The bullet hits Jason in the chest.

163

Jason is pushed back a foot and looks at Desdemona, stunned.

"What the fuck?" he says.

Crystal picks up the butcher knife on the counter and stabs down to kill the baby while the others are distracted. Before the knife can reach the baby, Desdemona fires another shot. It hits Crystal in the belly and she flies backwards onto the floor.

"You fucking bitch," Jason says.

He rushes her with his machete raised but he is stopped short by a bullet in his heart. He looks down at the holes in his chest, confused by the blood leaking out of his body. Then his eyes close and he falls.

Crystal holds her belly. She can tell that the bullet killed the child growing inside of her. She punches the wall next to her, frustrated that she won't be able to kill it herself.

Desdemona picks the crying baby up from the table and puts it to her chest. She holds the rifle awkwardly with one arm, pointing it at her bleeding friend. She isn't sure what Crystal might do. The severed heads of the two gray creatures blink languidly at Desdemona.

"You fucking shot me," Crystal says. "You fucking killed my boyfriend!"

"I didn't have a choice," Desdemona says.

Crystal crawls across the floor towards Desdemona,

holding her stomach wound. Her face turns red. She begins to cry.

"I thought you were my best friend!" Crystal says.

Desdemona's eyes begin to tear. "I'm sorry."

"You'd kill me to save that *thing*," Crystal says.

Desdemona shakes her head. "It's just a baby."

"It's one of those things," Crystal says. "It would have killed people just like its parents."

"You don't know that," Desdemona says.

"Des . . ." Crystal says, stretching her arms to Desdemona as if praying to her.

"Crystal . . ." Desdemona says.

"Please . . ." Crystal begs, her face flooded with tears.

Crystal reaches out to Des's hands.

"Please . . ." Crystal continues. "Let me kill it."

Desdemona steps back, but Crystal lunges at the baby. She grabs Desdemona's hands and tries to pry the infant out of them.

"Just let me kill it," Crystal shrieks.

Des kicks her in the chest and points the rifle at her head. Then she pulls the trigger. It clicks. She's out of bullets. Crystal falls onto her butt and cries louder. She closes her eyes and begins to wail like a spoiled three-year-old.

They don't say anything to each other after that. Desdemona turns away from her. She drops the gun, passes Kevin's body in the entryway, then takes the baby out of the cabin into the woods.

Dawn is breaking. Desdemona is walking down the winding dirt road with a mangled baby in her arms. Her butterfly tattoos are coated with a film of dried blood. She is still wearing her muddy pink bra and panties. She is still barefoot. Since she can't feel much of anything anymore, she hasn't noticed that the bottoms of her feet have been torn apart against the rocks, leaving a trail of bloody footprints all the way down the mountain.

The infant has stopped crying and has gone limp. She holds it tightly against her abdomen. Its lower body is sliding inside of the hollow cavity where Desdemona's innards had been removed. Des feels as if she's floating. She can't tell if she's alive or dead.

There is a faint screaming sound echoing in the valley. Desdemona stops and looks back the way she came. She hears the yelling. Somebody is yelling and cursing at the top of their lungs. It sounds like Crystal.

The screams get louder. Desdemona waits until she sees Crystal come into view. Her friend is crazed, holding a machete over her head as she flies down the mountain. Crystal sees Desdemona and picks up speed. Her eyes so wide they are popping out of her face, her blonde hair is dreadlocked with blood. She is in a murderous rage. Desdemona can't tell if she is after just the baby or both of them.

Desdemona turns to run. She can't move as fast as Crystal with her bare feet, but she's far enough ahead to get to the bottom of the hill and escape into the woods before Crystal can catch up to her. She zigzags through trees, attempting to lose her friend.

The deranged cheerleader races through the forest after Desdemona, hacking at branches that get in her face. Words gurgle out of her lungs at Des, but they are unintelligible. Her dangling breast flaps so hard against her ribcage that it breaks off, tumbles out of her shirt, and plops onto the ground like a cow patty.

As Desdemona dashes through the woods, carrying the limp rag doll of a baby, she passes a deer with a shredded torso standing next to a tree. The deer is missing half of its side, its stomach a black hollow, its ribs jutting out of its bloody fur, as if the creature had been half-eaten by wolves. It just looks at Des as she passes, chewing on grass as though nothing is wrong with it.

Desdemona runs by other mutilated animals. A bird with a missing wing and a broken beak hops through the roots of an old tree, a skinless squirrel runs across a branch with a nut in its mouth, a pulverized skunk that looks like it had been flattened under the wheels of a bus slithers into the bushes like a furry stingray.

Crystal catches up to Des before she reaches the edge of the forest. She swings the machete into Desdemona's back and cuts through one of her butterfly wings. Desdemona doesn't feel it. She picks up the pace.

The highway is up ahead. Desdemona thinks if she can just get to the highway, she will be safe. Somebody will drive by and pick her up before Crystal can get them.

She hears a screaming in her ear as Crystal swings the knife again, clipping her skull.

Desdemona gets so close to the highway that she can see all the bodies. The road is littered with dozens of dead animals, the same ones they passed on the way up to the cabin. Dead deer and dead rabbits are piled high, rotting, covered with flies. Nobody ever bothered to clean them up.

Just as they get to the highway, Crystal raises the machete for another attack.

Desdemona dodges. She jumps out of the forest, over a dead dog, into the road. Then the light disappears out of her eyes. Her legs become rubber. She crumbles to the ground with the lifeless baby underneath her. Then she dies.

As Crystal chases after her into the highway, she also becomes limp and drops to the ground. The pain in her stomach becomes too incredible to bare. She curls up into a ball, on top of the rancid animal corpses. The machete slides out of her fingers. She closes her eyes tight and cries.

The sun is shining brightly in the sky by the time the law enforcement ranger drives casually down the road. An older man with a gray mustache and a bald head steps out of the vehicle.

Crystal opens her eyes to see his leathery brown lips frowning at her from above.

"Don't touch me," she tells him.

He doesn't move, just stands over her body.

"I don't like to be touched," she says, as the light fades out of her eyes.

EPILOGUE
ROY

Kevin wakes up.

He looks down to find a bronze hand sticking out of his chest. He wonders why he is hanging on the wall, impaled by such a tacky wall ornament. He also wonders why his heart is outside of his body, lying on the floor.

Kevin looks out of the door into the woods and absorbs the cool morning air. Birds are tweeting in the trees outside. He would have thought it was a beautiful day, had he not been impaled.

"Why am I not dead?" Kevin says.

He looks towards the living room, but he can't see much. He isn't sure if anyone is in there.

"Hey," he says louder, to see if anyone can hear. "I'm still alive."

He hears a grunt.

Jason opens his eyes and rubs his forehead.

"Yeah," Jason says. "I'm alive, too."

"What the fuck's going on?" Kevin says. "What was that thing that did this to me? Why am I still alive?"

Jason puts his finger in a bullet hole. He can't really feel the bullets inside of him. He's not in any pain.

"Who the hell knows," Jason says, taking a swig of scotch.

Jason goes upstairs and puts on some pants. He steps out on the balcony. He lights a cigarette and looks out over the vast forest. Then he takes another swig of scotch.

Inside the cabin, Kevin says, "Can you get me down?"

Jason can't hear him.

"Hello?" Kevin says. "I'm kind of stuck."

Kevin tries to get himself down, but he can't get the thumb of the bronze hand back in through the hole. So he just hangs there for a while, waiting for Jason to come back to let him down.

He sees something coming out of the woods towards him. It is Stephanie. She staggers like a zombie into the cabin and smiles up at the hanging man.

"There you are," Stephanie says.

"Stephanie," Kevin says. "You're still alive, too? Are you okay?"

Stephanie sways back and forth at him, her eyes rolling around in her head.

"Can you help me down?" Kevin says.

She just sways at him.

"Steph," Kevin says. "Are you okay?"

She looks up at him. "Kevin . . ." Then she wraps her arms around him.

"Thanks, Steph," he says. "Now if you can just lift me up a little I think I could be able to slide this thing out of me."

Stephanie caresses his sides.

"Kevin . . ." She kisses his nipple through his shirt. "I love you. I've always loved you."

Stephanie pulls his pants down.

"What are you doing?" Kevin says.

"I want you," she says, while removing her own pants.

She climbs up the bronze hands and rubs her body against Kevin's penis until it becomes aroused.

"Let me down," Kevin says.

She opens her lips to kiss him but he moves his head back. Inside of her mouth, he can see light from the sun shining through the bullet hole on the other side of her head.

"Are those teeth?" Kevin says, as Stephanie forces his penis inside of her.

Stephanie's vaginal teeth scrape against him as she makes love to him. Kevin cringes as she presses her messy head wound against his cheek. He doesn't enjoy the sex. It feels like he's getting a really bad blowjob from a girl with big teeth and a small mouth.

The law enforcement ranger enters the cabin and sees the teenaged girl with half a skull fucking the impaled teenaged boy against the wall.

He takes off his sunglasses and sighs at them.

Kevin sees the man over Stephanie's shoulder.

"Can you get her off me and help me down?" Kevin says.

The law enforcement ranger doesn't say anything. He walks past him into the living room. He sees the gray body parts scattered around the room. Then he notices the lobster boy's head hanging from the wall, staring at him.

"Looks like you finally got what was coming to you," the ranger says to the severed head. His voice is low and gruff. "You sorry son of a bitch."

Jason comes down the stairs. He drinks his scotch and leans against the wall.

"You the Nolan boy?" the ranger asks.

"Yeah," Jason says.

"You're going to have to come with me."

The forest ranger's name is Roy. He's the only ranger responsible for this region. None of the other rangers are willing to go anywhere near it.

"There's something funny about these woods," Roy says. "People who come here seem to have a lot of difficulty dying."

Roy takes Stephanie and Kevin off of the walls. He has Jason take all of the mutant body parts and pile them into a wheelbarrow.

"Can you take us to the hospital?" Kevin asks.

The ranger shakes his head.

"You can never leave," the ranger says. "If you leave this land you will die."

The ranger tells them about Desdemona and Crystal. They died because they left the forest.

"Unless you want to end up like them, you better come with me."

Rick is up in a tree. He is still skewered by a vertical pine branch, piercing his vagina, through his body, and out of his mouth. All night, he had been trying to climb the branch. He would pull himself up with both hands, the bark of the branch ripping against his tongue and his internal organs, but before he could get to the top his strength would give out and he would slide all the way back down. Then he would try again.

They go to retrieve Rick after Jason told Roy what had happened to him. Roy insisted that Rick was still alive up there. He was right. They chop down the branch that impaled Rick and then slide it out of him as quickly as they can. Roy doesn't care about damaging his internal organs.

"You're already dead," he tells Rick. "You don't need your insides no more."

177

Rick can't speak. He nods his head as the messy pulp that was once his internal organs leaks out of his vagina.

Roy leads the four teenagers deeper into the woods. They have supplies from the cabin packed up in bags slung over their shoulders. Jason pushes the wheelbarrow full of body parts behind the ranger.

He takes them to a small village up in the hills. It is a collection of shacks and run down cabins. The villagers come out of their homes to greet them. They stagger slowly, raising their arms out to the teenagers.

"They are like you," Roy says. "They died in this forest and can never leave."

Kevin notices their flesh. All of them are mutilated. They have had limbs severed and sewn back on. They have missing pieces of meat. They are deformed and mangled, like living road kill.

Jason and Kevin watch as the deranged freaks swarm around them. They reach out their hands and caress the teenagers' bodies. They moan and wheeze at the newcomers as they feel them. The young men recoil from the villagers, as if they are lepers.

The forest ranger pushes on their backs and cracks a smile.

"Welcome to your new home," he says.

ABOUT THE AUTHOR

Carlton Mellick III is one of the leading authors in the new *Bizarro* genre uprising. Since 2001, his surreal counterculture novels have drawn an international cult following despite the fact that they have been shunned by most libraries and corporate bookstores. He lives in Portland, OR, where he is well-known for his DMing (Dungeon Mastering) skills.

Visit him online at **www.avantpunk.com**

the AVANT PUNK BOOK CLUB

SUBSCRIBE NOW!

Tired of trying to track down books by Carlton Mellick III? Sick of the long wait from amazon.com or bugging Barnes and Noble to actually put the rotten things on their shelves? Then you should subscribe to **The Avant Punk Book Club!** For $55, you will get the next six Carlton Mellick III books released through Avant Punk sent directly to your home *one month before their release dates!* No more waiting, no more hassle. Just razor wire butt plugs all year round!

Please fill out the form and mail it to the address below with a check or money order for $55 made out to Rose O'Keefe. You can also pay online via paypal.com to publisher@eraserheadpress.com, just put "Avant Punk Book Club" in the subject line. NOTE: these books will be released on an irregular basis, but CM3 is shooting for a bi-monthly writing schedule. There might also be the occasional Mellick-approved guest Bizarro author book released through the Avant Punk Book Club, but no more than one or two of the six.

Rose O'Keefe / Eraserhead Press
205 NE Bryant
Portland, OR 97211

Name_____

Address_____

City_____ State_____ Zip_____

Bizarro books

CATALOG   SPRING 2010

Bizarro Books publishes under the following imprints:

www.rawdogscreamingpress.com

www.eraserheadpress.com

www.afterbirthbooks.com

www.swallowdownpress.com

For all your Bizarro needs visit:

WWW.BIZARROCENTRAL.COM

Introduce yourselves to the bizarro genre and all of its authors with the Bizarro Starter Kit series. Each volume features short novels and short stories by ten of the leading bizarro authors, designed to give you a perfect sampling of the genre for only $5 plus shipping.

BB-0X1
"The Bizarro Starter Kit" (Orange)

Featuring D. Harlan Wilson, Carlton Mellick III, Jeremy Robert Johnson, Kevin L Donihe, Gina Ranalli, Andre Duza, Vincent W. Sakowski, Steve Beard, John Edward Lawson, and Bruce Taylor.

236 pages $5

BB-0X2
"The Bizarro Starter Kit" (Blue)

Featuring Ray Fracalossy, Jeremy C. Shipp, Jordan Krall, Mykle Hansen, Andersen Prunty, Eckhard Gerdes, Bradley Sands, Steve Aylett, Christian TeBordo, and Tony Rauch.

244 pages $5

BB-001 "The Kafka Effekt" D. Harlan Wilson - A collection of forty-four irreal short stories loosely written in the vein of Franz Kafka, with more than a pinch of William S. Burroughs sprinkled on top. **211 pages $14**

BB-002 "Satan Burger" Carlton Mellick III - The cult novel that put Carlton Mellick III on the map ... Six punks get jobs at a fast food restaurant owned by the devil in a city violently overpopulated by surreal alien cultures. **236 pages $14**

BB-003 "Some Things Are Better Left Unplugged" Vincent Sakwoski - Join The Man and his Nemesis, the obese tabby, for a nightmare roller coaster ride into this postmodern fantasy. **152 pages $10**

BB-004 "Shall We Gather At the Garden?" Kevin L Donihe - Donihe's Debut novel. Midgets take over the world, The Church of Lionel Richie vs. The Church of the Byrds, plant porn and more! **244 pages $14**

BB-005 "Razor Wire Pubic Hair" Carlton Mellick III - A genderless humandildo is purchased by a razor dominatrix and brought into her nightmarish world of bizarre sex and mutilation. **176 pages $11**

BB-006 "Stranger on the Loose" D. Harlan Wilson - The fiction of Wilson's 2nd collection is planted in the soil of normalcy, but what grows out of that soil is a dark, witty, otherworldly jungle... **228 pages $14**

BB-007 "The Baby Jesus Butt Plug" Carlton Mellick III - Using clones of the Baby Jesus for anal sex will be the hip sex fetish of the future. **92 pages $10**

BB-008 "Fishyfleshed" Carlton Mellick III - The world of the past is an illogical flatland lacking in dimension and color, a sick-scape of crispy squid people wandering the desert for no apparent reason. **260 pages $14**

BB-009 **"Dead Bitch Army" Andre Duza** - Step into a world filled with racist teenagers, cannibals, 100 warped Uncle Sams, automobiles with razor-sharp teeth, living graffiti, and a pissed-off zombie bitch out for revenge. **344 pages $16**

BB-010 **"The Menstruating Mall" Carlton Mellick III** - "The Breakfast Club meets Chopping Mall as directed by David Lynch." - Brian Keene **212 pages $12**

BB-011 **"Angel Dust Apocalypse" Jeremy Robert Johnson** - Meth-heads, man-made monsters, and murderous Neo-Nazis. "Seriously amazing short stories..." - Chuck Palahniuk, author of Fight Club **184 pages $11**

BB-012 **"Ocean of Lard" Kevin L Donihe / Carlton Mellick III** - A parody of those old Choose Your Own Adventure kid's books about some very odd pirates sailing on a sea made of animal fat. **176 pages $12**

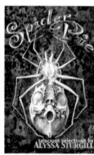

BB-013 **"Last Burn in Hell" John Edward Lawson** - From his lurid angst-affair with a lesbian music diva to his ascendance as unlikely pop icon the one constant for Kenrick Brimley, official state prison gigolo, is he's got no clue what he's doing. **172 pages $14**

BB-014 **"Tangerinephant" Kevin Dole 2** - TV-obsessed aliens have abducted Michael Tangerinephant in this bizarro combination of science fiction, satire, and surrealism. **164 pages $11**

BB-015 **"Foop!" Chris Genoa** - Strange happenings are going on at Dactyl, Inc, the world's first and only time travel tourism company.

"A surreal pie in the face!" - Christopher Moore **300 pages $14**

BB-016 **"Spider Pie" Alyssa Sturgill** - A one-way trip down a rabbit hole inhabited by sexual deviants and friendly monsters, fairytale beginnings and hideous endings. **104 pages $11**

BB-017 "The Unauthorized Woman" Efrem Emerson - Enter the world of the inner freak, a landscape populated by the pre-dead and morticioners, by cockroaches and 300-lb robots. **104 pages $11**

BB-018 "Fugue XXIX" Forrest Aguirre - Tales from the fringe of speculative literary fiction where innovative minds dream up the future's uncharted territories while mining forgotten treasures of the past. **220 pages $16**

BB-019 "Pocket Full of Loose Razorblades" John Edward Lawson - A collection of dark bizarro stories. From a giant rectum to a foot-fungus factory to a girl with a biforked tongue. **190 pages $13**

BB-020 "Punk Land" Carlton Mellick III - In the punk version of Heaven, the anarchist utopia is threatened by corporate fascism and only Goblin, Mortician's sperm, and a blue-mohawked female assassin named Shark Girl can stop them. **284 pages $15**

BB-021 "Pseudo-City" D. Harlan Wilson - Pseudo-City exposes what waits in the bathroom stall, under the manhole cover and in the corporate boardroom, all in a way that can only be described as mind-bogglingly irreal. **220 pages $16**

BB-022 "Kafka's Uncle and Other Strange Tales" Bruce Taylor - Anslenot and his giant tarantula (tormentor? fri-end?) wander a desecrated world in this novel and collection of stories from Mr. Magic Realism Himself. **348 pages $17**

BB-023 "Sex and Death In Television Town" Carlton Mellick III - In the old west, a gang of hermaphrodite gunslingers take refuge from a demon plague in Telos: a town where its citizens have televisions instead of heads. **184 pages $12**

BB-024 "It Came From Below The Belt" Bradley Sands - What can Grover Goldstein do when his severed, sentient penis forces him to return to high school and help it win the presidential election? **204 pages $13**

BB-025 "Sick: An Anthology of Illness" John Lawson, editor - These Sick stories are horrendous and hilarious dissections of creative minds on the scalpel's edge. **296 pages $16**

BB-026 "Tempting Disaster" John Lawson, editor - A shocking and alluring anthology from the fringe that examines our culture's obsession with taboos. **260 pages $16**

BB-027 "Siren Promised" Jeremy Robert Johnson - Nominated for the Bram Stoker Award. A potent mix of bad drugs, bad dreams, brutal bad guys, and surreal/incredible art by Alan M. Clark. **190 pages $13**

BB-028 "Chemical Gardens" Gina Ranalli - Ro and punk band Green is the Enemy find Kreepkins, a surfer-dude warlock, a vengeful demon, and a Metal Priestess in their way as they try to escape an underground nightmare. **188 pages $13**

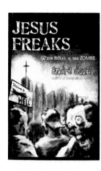   

BB-029 "Jesus Freaks" Andre Duza - For God so loved the world that he gave his only two begotten sons… and a few million zombies. **400 pages $16**

BB-030 "Grape City" Kevin L. Donihe - More Donihe-style comedic bizarro about a demon named Charles who is forced to work a minimum wage job on Earth after Hell goes out of business. **108 pages $10**

BB-031 "Sea of the Patchwork Cats" Carlton Mellick III - A quiet dreamlike tale set in the ashes of the human race. For Mellick enthusiasts who also adore The Twilight Zone. **112 pages $10**

BB-032 "Extinction Journals" Jeremy Robert Johnson - An uncanny voyage across a newly nuclear America where one man must confront the problems associated with loneliness, insane dieties, radiation, love, and an ever-evolving cockroach suit with a mind of its own. **104 pages $10**

  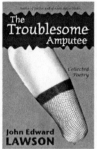 

BB-033 **"Meat Puppet Cabaret" Steve Beard** - At last! The secret connection between Jack the Ripper and Princess Diana's death revealed! **240 pages $16 / $30**

BB-034 **"The Greatest Fucking Moment in Sports" Kevin L. Donihe** - In the tradition of the surreal anti-sitcom Get A Life comes a tale of triumph and agape love from the master of comedic bizarro. **108 pages $10**

BB-035 **"The Troublesome Amputee" John Edward Lawson** - Disturbing verse from a man who truly believes nothing is sacred and intends to prove it. **104 pages $9**

BB-036 **"Deity" Vic Mudd** - God (who doesn't like to be called "God") comes down to a typical, suburban, Ohio family for a little vacation—but it doesn't turn out to be as relaxing as He had hoped it would be... **168 pages $12**

BB-037 **"The Haunted Vagina" Carlton Mellick III** - It's difficult to love a woman whose vagina is a gateway to the world of the dead. **132 pages $10**

BB-038 **"Tales from the Vinegar Wasteland" Ray Fracalossy** - Witness: a man is slowly losing his face, a neighbor who periodically screams out for no apparent reason, and a house with a room that doesn't actually exist. **240 pages $14**

BB-039 **"Suicide Girls in the Afterlife" Gina Ranalli** - After Pogue commits suicide, she unexpectedly finds herself an unwilling "guest" at a hotel in the Afterlife, where she meets a group of bizarre characters, including a goth Satan, a hippie Jesus, and an alien-human hybrid. **100 pages $9**

BB-040 **"And Your Point Is?" Steve Aylett** - In this follow-up to LINT multiple authors provide critical commentary and essays about Jeff Lint's mind-bending literature. **104 pages $11**

BB-041 **"Not Quite One of the Boys" Vincent Sakowski** - While drug-dealer Maxi drinks with Dante in purgatory, God and Satan play a little tri-level chess and do a little bargaining over his business partner, Vinnie, who is still left on earth. **220 pages $14**

BB-042 **"Teeth and Tongue Landscape" Carlton Mellick III** - On a planet made out of meat, a socially-obsessive monophobic man tries to find his place amongst the strange creatures and communities that he comes across. **110 pages $10**

BB-043 **"War Slut" Carlton Mellick III** - Part "1984," part "Waiting for Godot," and part action horror video game adaptation of John Carpenter's "The Thing." **116 pages $10**

BB-044 **"All Encompassing Trip" Nicole Del Sesto** - In a world where coffee is no longer available, the only television shows are reality TV re-runs, and the animals are talking back, Nikki, Amber and a singing Coyote in a do-rag are out to restore the light **308 pages $15**

BB-045 **"Dr. Identity" D. Harlan Wilson** - Follow the Dystopian Duo on a killing spree of epic proportions through the irreal postcapitalist city of Bliptown where time ticks sideways, artificial Bug-Eyed Monsters punish citizens for consumer-capitalist lethargy, and ultraviolence is as essential as a daily multivitamin. **208 pages $15**

BB-046 **"The Million-Year Centipede" Eckhard Gerdes** - Wakelin, frontman for 'The Hinge,' wrote a poem so prophetic that to ignore it dooms a person to drown in blood. **130 pages $12**

BB-047 **"Sausagey Santa" Carlton Mellick III** - A bizarro Christmas tale featuring Santa as a piratey mutant with a body made of sausages. 124 pages $10

BB-048 **"Misadventures in a Thumbnail Universe" Vincent Sakowski** - Dive deep into the surreal and satirical realms of neo-classical Blender Fiction, filled with television shoes and flesh-filled skies. **120 pages $10**

BB-049 **"Vacation" Jeremy C. Shipp** - Blueblood Bernard Johnson leaved his boring life behind to go on The Vacation, a year-long corporate sponsored odyssey. But instead of seeing the world, Bernard is captured by terrorists, becomes a key figure in secret drug wars, and, worse, doesn't once miss his secure American Dream. **160 pages $14**

BB-051 **"13 Thorns" Gina Ranalli** - Thirteen tales of twisted, bizarro horror. **240 pages $13**

BB-050 **"Discouraging at Best" John Edward Lawson** - A collection where the absurdity of the mundane expands exponentially creating a tidal wave that sweeps reason away. For those who enjoy satire, bizarro, or a good old-fashioned slap to the senses. **208 pages $15**

BB-052 **"Better Ways of Being Dead" Christian TeBordo** - In this class, the students have to keep one palm down on the table at all times, and listen to lectures about a panda who speaks Chinese. **216 pages $14**

BB-053 **"Ballad of a Slow Poisoner" Andrew Goldfarb** Millford Mutterwurst sat down on a Tuesday to take his afternoon tea, and made the unpleasant discovery that his elbows were becoming flatter. **128 pages $10**

BB-054 **"Wall of Kiss" Gina Ranalli** - A woman... A wall... Sometimes love blooms in the strangest of places. **108 pages $9**

BB-055 **"HELP! A Bear is Eating Me" Mykle Hansen** - The bizarro, heartwarming, magical tale of poor planning, hubris and severe blood loss... **150 pages $11**

BB-056 **"Piecemeal June" Jordan Krall** - A man falls in love with a living sex doll, but with love comes danger when her creator comes after her with crab-squid assassins. **90 pages $9**

BB-057 "Laredo" Tony Rauch - Dreamlike, surreal stories by Tony Rauch. **180 pages $12**

BB-058 "The Overwhelming Urge" Andersen Prunty - A collection of bizarro tales by Andersen Prunty. **150 pages $11**

BB-059 "Adolf in Wonderland" Carlton Mellick III - A dreamlike adventure that takes a young descendant of Adolf Hitler's design and sends him down the rabbit hole into a world of imperfection and disorder. **180 pages $11**

BB-060 "Super Cell Anemia" Duncan B. Barlow - "Unrelentingly bizarre and mysterious, unsettling in all the right ways..." - Brian Evenson. **180 pages $12**

 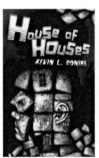  

BB-061 "Ultra Fuckers" Carlton Mellick III - Absurdist suburban horror about a couple who enter an upper middle class gated community but can't find their way out. **108 pages $9**

BB-062 "House of Houses" Kevin L. Donihe - An odd man wants to marry his house. Unfortunately, all of the houses in the world collapse at the same time in the Great House Holocaust. Now he must travel to House Heaven to find his departed fiancee. **172 pages $11**

BB-063 "Necro Sex Machine" Andre Duza - The Dead Bicth returns in this follow-up to the bizarro zombie epic Dead Bitch Army. **400 pages $16**

BB-064 "Squid Pulp Blues" Jordan Krall - In these three bizarro-noir novellas, the reader is thrown into a world of murderers, drugs made from squid parts, deformed gun-toting veterans, and a mischievous apocalyptic donkey. **204 pages $12**

BB-065 **"Jack and Mr. Grin" Andersen Prunty** - "When Mr. Grin calls you can hear a smile in his voice. Not a warm and friendly smile, but the kind that seizes your spine in fear. You don't need to pay your phone bill to hear it. That smile is in every line of Prunty's prose." - Tom Bradley. **208 pages $12**

BB-066 **"Cybernetrix" Carlton Mellick III** - What would you do if your normal everyday world was slowly mutating into the video game world from Tron? **212 pages $12**

BB-067 **"Lemur" Tom Bradley** - Spencer Sproul is a would-be serial-killing bus boy who can't manage to murder, injure, or even scare anybody. However, there are other ways to do damage to far more people and do it legally... **120 pages $12**

BB-068 **"Cocoon of Terror" Jason Earls** - Decapitated corpses...a sculpture of terror...Zelian's masterpiece, his Cocoon of Terror, will trigger a supernatural disaster for everyone on Earth. **196 pages $14**

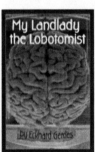

BB-069 **"Mother Puncher" Gina Ranalli** - The world has become tragically over-populated and now the government strongly opposes procreation. Ed is employed by the government as a mother-puncher. He doesn't relish his job, but he knows it has to be done and he knows he's the best one to do it. **120 pages $9**

BB-070 **"My Landlady the Lobotomist" Eckhard Gerdes** - The brains of past tenants line the shelves of my boarding house, soaking in a mysterious elixir. One more slip-up and the landlady might just add my frontal lobe to her collection. **116 pages $12**

BB-071 **"CPR for Dummies" Mickey Z.** - This hilarious freakshow at the world's end is the fragmented, sobering debut novel by acclaimed nonfiction author Mickey Z. **216 pages $14**

BB-072 **"Zerostrata" Andersen Prunty** - Hansel Nothing lives in a tree house, suffers from memory loss, has a very eccentric family, and falls in love with a woman who runs naked through the woods every night. **144 pages $11**

ORDER FORM

TITLES	QTY	PRICE	TOTAL

Please make checks and moneyorders payable to ROSE O'KEEFE / BIZARRO BOOKS in U.S. funds only. Please don't send bad checks! Allow 2-6 weeks for delivery. International orders may take longer. If you'd like to pay online via PAYPAL.COM, send payments to publisher@eraserheadpress.com.

SHIPPING: US ORDERS - $2 for the first book, $1 for each additional book. For priority shipping, add an additional $4. INT'L ORDERS - $5 for the first book, $3 for each additional book. Add an additional $5 per book for global priority shipping.

Send payment to:

BIZARRO BOOKS
  C/O Rose O'Keefe
  205 NE Bryant
  Portland, OR 97211

Address		
City	State	Zip
Email	Phone